Will's Story
1771

More stories in the

YOUNG AMERICANS

Colonial Williamsburg

SERIES BY JOAN LOWERY NIXON

ANN'S STORY: 1747
CAESAR'S STORY: 1759
NANCY'S STORY: 1765

YOUNG AMERICANS

Colonial Williamsburg

Will's Story
1771

JOAN LOWERY NIXON

Delacorte Press

Published by
Delacorte Press
an imprint of
Random House Children's Books
a division of Random House, Inc.
1540 Broadway
New York, New York 10036

Visit us on the Web! www.randomhouse.com/kids
Educators and librarians, for a variety of teaching tools, visit us at www.randomhouse.com/teachers

Cataloging-in-Publication Data is available from the Library of Congress.
ISBN: 0-385-32682-3

The text of this book is set in 12-point Minion.
Book design by Patrice Sheridan
Manufactured in the United States of America
April 2001
10 9 8 7 6 5 4 3 2 1
BVG

Contents

A LETTER FROM THE

COLONIAL WILLIAMSBURG

FOUNDATION

Will Pelham was a real boy who lived in Williamsburg, Virginia, in the 1770s. His father, Peter Pelham, was organist at Bruton Parish Church. Although a talented musician and teacher, Mr. Pelham needed additional money to support his large family. He supplemented his income by serving as keeper of the long-standing public gaol. Construction of the public gaol began in 1701, with debtors' cells added in 1711 and gaoler's quarters built in 1722.

Today the public gaol is part of Colonial Williamsburg, a living history museum. It, along with the rest of Colonial Williamsburg's Historic Area, has been restored to the way it was during the American Revolution. People in costume tell the story of Virginia's contribution to American independence and show visitors life in the colonial era.

At Colonial Williamsburg, you can see where Will lived and visit the public gaol. You can visit the courthouse and the Capitol to learn about colonial laws and trials. And you can stop in at the Raleigh Tavern, where Will, Joseph, and Robert spoke to George Washington.

The Colonial Williamsburg Foundation is proud to have worked with Joan Lowery Nixon on the Young Americans series. Staff members met with Mrs. Nixon and identified sources for her research. People at Colonial Williamsburg read each book to make sure it was as accurate as possible, from the way the characters speak to what they eat to the clothes they wear. Mrs. Nixon's note at the end of the book tells exactly what we know about Will, his family, and his friends.

Another way to learn more about the life of Will Pelham and his family and friends is to experience Williamsburg for yourself. A visit to Colonial Williamsburg is a journey to the past—we invite you to join us on that journey and bring history to life.

Cary Carson

Cary Carson
Vice President—Research
The Colonial Williamsburg Foundation

Prologue

"Mrs. Otts has closed her stall," Lori Smith called to her friend Keisha Martin. "Hurry! Before she leaves!"

As Lori and Keisha raced across Colonial Williamsburg's Nicholson Street to Market Square, they saw Molly Otts spread her long, full skirts and settle on a bench in the late-afternoon shade.

Mrs. Otts smiled when she saw Lori and Keisha. " 'Tis good to take a few moments' rest near the end of a warm day such as this," she said.

Lori smiled in return. "Hi, Mrs. Otts," she said. "We came to hear your story about Will Pelham."

Mrs. Otts hesitated. "Perhaps another time. Don't the young lads wish to hear the story, too?"

"It's okay. Here they come now," Keisha said. She jumped up and down, waving and shouting "Hurry

1

up!" at Chip Hahn, Stewart Dowling, and Halim Jordan.

As the entire group flopped down on the grass in front of Mrs. Otts's bench, Stewart said, "Mrs. Otts, you told us the Pelham family lived in the public gaol. How could any family live in a gaol with murderers and thieves?"

"I'm certain it must have been very difficult for them and even worrisome at times," Mrs. Otts answered. "It must have been frightening, too, for John and Sarah, who had to pass the cells at night to reach the stairs to the large bedchamber they shared with twelve-year-old Will. It certainly frightened Will."

"We saw a portrait of his grandfather Pelham," Lori said. "Did Will look like his father's side of the family?"

"No, he looked more like his mother, Ann, with his light brown hair and brown eyes, but, like his father, Will had a great fondness for music and books."

Stewart looked puzzled. "We were told that Peter Pelham was a famous organist and even a composer. I don't understand. Why did he want to be a gaoler, too?"

"Mr. Pelham and his wife had five children living with them when he applied for the position of gaoler," Mrs. Otts answered. "He gave concerts and lessons on the harpsichord, spinet, and organ, in addition to performing his regular occupation as organist at Bruton Parish Church. He also served as clerk to committees of the House of Burgesses, as well as to both Governor Fauquier and Governor Botetourt. Unfortunately, the money he received for all this work was not enough to support his family. The occupation of gaoler, to which Mr. Pelham were appointed in 1771, fulfilled this need."

Lori leaned forward as she said, "You told us something about one of the prisoners—a horse thief named Jake."

"And a pirate ghost," Chip added.

"And Will getting into trouble," Halim said.

Mrs. Otts held up her hands and laughed. "Pray do not be so impatient," she said. "Make yourselves comfortable, listen, and I'll tell you Will Pelham's story."

Chapter One

Will Pelham's candlestick trembled in his hand as he stepped silently and carefully. Around him the flickering light threw deep shadows up the walls of the passage. More than two months had passed since July 15, 1771, the day his father had posted bond as gaoler and had moved his family into the living quarters attached to the public gaol. Even though Will knew by now he should be used to passing the criminals' cells to reach the stairs, he still dreaded his nightly walk to the upstairs bedchamber he shared with his older sister and younger brother.

From the darkness of the cells came a low mumble. Will started and pressed himself against the wall, holding his breath. He listened intently and soon realized that what he had heard was nothing more than one of the prisoners talking in his sleep.

Another prisoner stirred, his chains rattling as he shifted on the pile of straw that served as his bed. Will shuddered. He would never get used to that horrible sound.

He hadn't minded the small, cramped house he and his family had lived in before coming here. And he hadn't once complained when a meal or two had been slight, without so much as a slice of meat. He'd gladly return to the way they had lived before they'd moved to the public gaol—even to wearing mended shirts with frayed seams—if Papa would only give up this terrible job of gaoler.

Will sighed, knowing it would never happen. His father was grateful for the extra income. "What I am given as organist for Bruton Parish Church and for the harpsichord lessons I teach is not enough to support my family," he had explained. "We should all consider the position of gaoler as good fortune that has come our way. Even our friends rejoice for us."

Will's mother had agreed, saying, "At least these living quarters are better than those we had before."

This was true, Will admitted to himself. The new rooms in the building that housed the public gaol consisted of a large hall and bedchamber downstairs and a good-sized bedchamber upstairs. But neither of his parents had to walk this frightening passage every night after dark.

Will straightened, stepping away from the support of the wall, and steadied his candle, but he had taken only two steps before a low voice whispered from the darkness, "Hssst! Will!"

"What? Who?" Will cried, nearly dropping his candle.

"Not so loud. Keep your voice down," the voice said. "Come to the window in the cell door, Will."

Will did as he had been told, holding the candle high. Staring at him was a prisoner whose gray hair was matted and whose linen shirt and breeches were badly stained. The old man clung with both hands to the metal bars on the window in the door of the men's cell.

Wrinkling his nose at the smell, Will wondered when this prisoner had last bathed. He must have been brought to the jail this very day, because Will had not seen him before. "Who are you? How do you know my name?" Will asked.

"My name is Jake Sample," the man answered. "I heard you called Will by your father." He wiggled his fingers through the bars. "Pray come closer. I am lonely and unable to sleep. I must talk to someone."

Will hesitated, unwilling to step any closer. Even though he helped his father by bringing the prisoners water and their one meal of the day—pushing the plates of cornmeal mush called hominy and occasional scraps of meat through the food slot in the cell door—he rarely spoke with them.

He had tried to the best of his ability to answer the prisoners' questions if they asked about the welfare of their families or how long it would be until the next court would convene and their cases would be tried. He had hurried to get his father when they asked for medicine to stop the wracking coughs that came from sleeping on the drafty floor.

But those few conversations had taken place during daylight hours, and Will was not eager to speak with a prisoner who whispered from the darkness, beckoning with gnarled fingers. However, Will had been taught by his father always to keep in mind their responsibility for the prisoners' care, so he asked, "Are you not well, Mr. Sample?"

"I am well enough, thank you," Jake answered. He cocked his head, and his eyes narrowed and slid toward the darkness behind him. Lowering his voice even more, he said, "But Edward Teach isn't."

"Edward Teach?" Will had studied the roster of prisoners, and he didn't recognize that name.

"Edward Teach—Blackbeard the pirate!" Jake answered. "Fifteen of his men were held in this gaol. Thirteen of them were sentenced and hanged. Blackbeard's still mighty angry about that."

Chills shot up Will's backbone. He'd heard tales from his father about the pirate Blackbeard, who in the early 1700s terrorized ships traveling to and from the colonies. He knew that what Jake had said about Blackbeard's crew was true. But how could Jake know how Blackbeard felt? The pirate had been killed by the British more than fifty years before.

"I don't think he's feeling much of anything now. Everyone knows Blackbeard's dead!" Will blurted out.

Jake nodded solemnly, although his mouth twitched and his eyes glittered in the candlelight as if he were laughing. He slowly whispered, "I didn't say he was alive."

Will gasped and bolted down the passage—not toward the stairs to his bedchamber, but into the two downstairs rooms of the house set aside for the gaoler and his family.

Will's mother and sisters had already retired. Nellie, one of the family's slaves, had gone to her basement room, and Toby, their other slave, had banked the fire. But Will's father was still in the hall, writing in a ledger at his small desk in the corner.

"Papa!" Will called to his startled father. Will told him everything Jake Sample had said, then cried out, "Mr. Sample talks to ghosts!"

Peter Pelham rested his hands on Will's shoulders. "Do not alarm yourself, son," he said. "Think about what you just told me. Why did Mr. Sample say he wished to speak to you?"

Will blinked in surprise. "He said he was lonely and couldn't sleep, but—"

"Exactly," Mr. Pelham interrupted. "Then 'tis likely, since he had nothing to do and no one to talk to, he wished to have a bit of fun with you."

"You mean he deliberately wished to frighten me?" Will frowned. "I don't think that's something to laugh about."

"Old Jake Sample is harmless," Mr. Pelham said. "His neighbors claim that even though his mind wanders at times, he's not capable of hurting anyone."

Still upset, Will grumbled, "If he's harmless, then why is he in the gaol?"

"Jake was arrested for stealing a horse. The justices in his home county decided there was enough evidence against him to send him here to await trial."

"He stole a horse?" Will's anger quickly changed to a deep sorrow for the old man. Will knew that the penalty for horse theft was death by hanging.

"Fortunately for Jake, 'twas some doubt that the horse was stolen," Mr. Pelham said. "The horse's owner accused Jake, so Jake was arrested. But Jake claims the horse had escaped from its pasture and was wandering on the road. The mud on the road was deep—which made it difficult to walk, and Jake was a long way from home. He simply saw the horse's presence as a gift from heaven. He rode the horse to his home, stabled him, and groomed him. He even fed him. Jake claimed he planned to search for the horse's owner later."

Will heard the conviction in his father's voice. "You believe him, don't you, Papa?"

Mr. Pelham nodded. "His story is believable, and there are neighbors who will testify on Jake's behalf. When he comes to trial there is a good chance he'll be acquitted."

Will was glad of that. Jake was old, his body twisted and stooped. Yet like the other prisoners, he had to sleep in the unheated cell with nothing but a pile of straw to serve as a bed, and the night air through the barred window could be chill.

Perhaps Jake had simply been teasing him, as Papa thought. On the other hand, could the gaol still be haunted by Blackbeard's angry ghost? Could Jake actually hear a voice the rest of them couldn't hear? Will didn't want to find out.

Will followed his father's orders to go to his bed-chamber, but he continued to be troubled by Jake's words. As he reached the passage, he walked cautiously, holding his breath as he began to pass the criminals' cells.

"Hsst! Will!" came Jake's voice again, and fingers wiggled out from between the bars.

Will let out a yelp and broke into a run. Jake's raspy cackle of laughter followed him down the passage, stopping only when Will ran up the narrow flight of stairs and tightly shut the door.

The candlelight shone on the face of Will's eight-year-old brother, John, who was peacefully asleep, and Will was glad that Jake hadn't tried to frighten *him*.

"He'd best not," Will whispered as he tucked the blanket around John's shoulders.

Sarah, asleep in the bed across the large room, stirred and murmured, so Will blew out the candle. In the darkness he took off his shoes, stockings, and breeches before he climbed into his own bed.

As Will lay staring at the ceiling, still too wide awake to fall asleep, he thought about his two older brothers, Peter and Charles. A few months ago Peter had moved to New Brunswick County to become the county clerk. Charles, too, had moved to new lodgings. Will missed them. He wiggled uncomfortably in bed, wishing he were a few years older and could leave home to find employment, too.

He loved everyone in his family—his four brothers; his parents; and even his two sisters—seventeen-year-old Sarah, who could get awfully bossy when she felt like it, and six-year-old Elizabeth. Some of his favorite times were when he listened to his father play the organ in Bruton Parish Church and when they spent an evening as a family. Will's mother would quietly sew and his father would read aloud. But Will absolutely did not like living and working in the public gaol!

He remembered that when he had first complained about his chores at the gaol, his mother had said, "Understand our situation, Will. We have many mouths to feed." She glanced down and quietly added, "Your father must do what he can to care for his family. As the eldest son still living at home, you can be a big help to your father."

Will knew his brothers' absence left a lot of responsibility to him. And thinking about that didn't help him to sleep. He pulled the blanket up to his ears and squeezed his eyes shut. Unless he fell asleep soon, he wouldn't wake up early enough to read.

Will's favorite time of the day was early morning, when the sky was first growing light. He liked to curl into a chair next to the fireplace in the hall, where the fire was banked each night. He'd choose a favorite book, holding it close before he opened it, to breathe in the sharp, sour smell of ink on paper and the scent of the dark leather bindings, softer than his own skin. Then, carefully, he'd open the book to read. He loved the rough touch of the paper against his fingertips as he turned a page. But best of all he loved the words within the books.

He was often well into a story even before Toby entered the house to stir up the coals and build the fire. On rare occasions, if the fire had not been banked properly and had died out, Toby would reach into the cupboard next to the fireplace, take out the thin steel striker and the flint, and scrape with a scratching sound of metal against stone until sparks set the logs in the fireplace ablaze.

Thomas Gray's beautiful poetry, the fragrance of Nellie's cooking wafting up the stairs from the basement kitchen, the cozy warmth of the room . . . what could be finer? Will could forget that he lived in the public gaol, where prisoners groaned and mumbled and whispered in the darkness and talked to ghosts . . . but those moments were few.

Will squirmed, tangling the blanket. He didn't want to be the eldest son at home. He didn't want to help his father with the prisoners. And—above all—he didn't want to have to deal with a ghost!

Chapter Two

In the bright sunlit morning, Blackbeard's ghost seemed only a foolish notion. Will could almost laugh at the fearful way he'd raced down the passage the night before. *What's done is done*, he thought, and was no longer angry at Jake Sample for his strange way of poking fun.

Will had awakened too late for his quiet time to read before the others were up, so he had to get straight to work. Still a bit sleepy and very hungry, he picked up the prisoners' water bucket, which was kept outside the cells in the passage. He filled it with fresh water and returned to the women's cell. He handed the first cup to Alice Field through the bars of the cell. His father had told him that Miss Field had been imprisoned for a misdemeanor. Margaret Turnbull, the other woman in the cell, had been charged with grand larceny, a crime punishable by death.

Will was uncomfortable around the women prisoners. He spoke to them politely and with respect, as he had been taught to speak to all women. But these women were not like his mother or his mother's friends, who deserved respect. These women had committed crimes, and they were confined to a damp, cold cell until the time came for them to go to court.

Miss Field—who seemed more unkempt each day—constantly whined and sniffled. "How many days until the trials at General Court?" she asked Will.

Will counted on his fingers. "Twenty-three days. Today is Tuesday, September twenty-fourth. The court opens on Wednesday, October sixteenth."

Moaning, Miss Field stepped back, and Mrs. Turnbull took her place. At least Mrs. Turnbull kept her hair tucked inside her cap and managed to look tidy, Will thought.

As Mrs. Turnbull took her turn with the cup, she tried to reach through the bars to touch Will's face, but he flinched, stepping back out of reach. Her eyes were deep and sorrowful. "Once I had a son your age" was all she said.

When each woman had drunk her share of the water, Will lugged the heavy bucket to the passage outside the men's cell, where ten prisoners eagerly came to the bars.

A meager amount of light entered the cell from the barred window in the door leading to the exercise yard. In spite of the sunny day, the cell was dark and damp.

Will was familiar with the current list. His father had shown it to him the night before, after three new prisoners had arrived and had been registered. Besides Jake Sample, there were four others imprisoned for the felony of horse stealing: Samuel Flannagin, George Dutton, George Gray, and Thomas Welch. John Watts was in gaol for a misdemeanor committed in Williamsburg, John King for an unspecified felony in Spotsylvania, and Colin Campbell for the crime of maiming—also a felony—in Prince Edward County. Although all but John Watts had committed their crimes elsewhere in Virginia, they had been sent to Williamsburg's public gaol to await the October session of the General Court.

The prisoner named Emmanuel had been transferred the week before from a prison in a neighboring county. He had been held for two months after he'd been pointed out to a patroller by someone who had recognized him as a runaway slave. Tall, strong, and probably not much more than twenty years old, he'd refused to name his master or tell from where he'd escaped. He'd been brought to the public gaol, and a notice with his description had been posted in *The Virginia Gazette.* If his owner did not see the notice and claim him, Emmanuel would be hired out by Mr. Pelham to help defray the costs of his upkeep. This seemed fair enough to Will. As his father had explained to him, a slave knew he was the property of his owner, and running away was removing that property. It was the same thing as stealing.

Will was especially interested in one of the new prisoners who had been brought in the day before. His name was Mills Mansfield, and he'd been arrested for the crime of forgery, a felony. Mansfield, with his curly red hair, was taller than any of the others in the cell, so Will had no trouble recognizing him. Mansfield's clothes were not laborers' clothing such as most of the prisoners wore but were those of the middling sort. His breeches, shirt, and waistcoat were not made of the fine fabrics the gentry chose but of neat, serviceable cloth such as Will's father wore.

Jake was first in line for water. He grinned at Will, showing toothless gaps in his mouth. "Did you sleep well, lad?" he asked. His laugh soon turned into a raspy cough.

Will's face grew warm as he filled the cup with water and handed it to Jake. He desperately hoped that Jake wasn't going to tell the other men how Will had been frightened by tales of a pirate ghost.

He was relieved when Jake said no more about Blackbeard and simply downed the water in one long gulp. Will next handed the cup to a burly man, Thomas Welch, who roughly elbowed Jake aside as he grabbed the cup.

As Jake stumbled, making a sound of protest, Mr. Welch laughed and said, "We do not all have the gentlemanly manners of your Colonel George Washington."

Someone hooted at Jake, while others laughed. At the back of the group a man called, "Pray assure me we are not going to hear that story again."

Jake pushed up to the bars and looked into Will's eyes. " 'Tis not a story. 'Tis true," he said. "I once gave a cup of cold water to Colonel Washington himself when he stopped with his troops on the road by my house."

Again there were snickers. Will silently refilled the cup Mr. Welch handed him, allowing Jake to continue.

"Colonel Washington told me about his plans to defeat the French army," he said. "I spoke right up and told him to split his troops—to flank the French on two sides. Then double back and come in from the rear. Show those soldiers they were surrounded by the British." He smiled. "It's the way my dog and me herd the sheep into the barn each night."

Someone groaned, and Mr. Welch asked, "Just when did all this happen, old man?"

Jake squinted, his face crinkling up like greasy wrapping paper as he tried to think. "I don't rightly remember exactly when it took place. It may have been yesterday."

Colin Campbell reached for the filled cup and laughed loudly. "Nobody believes a single thing old Jake says," he told Will.

But Will watched Mills Mansfield smile and clap Jake on the shoulder. "That sounds like good advice," Mansfield said. "And Colonel Washington must have taken it, because the French army was defeated."

Jake grinned happily, his head bobbing up and down. He watched Mansfield accept a full cup of water from Will. Then he said, "I'm still thirsty."

Mansfield hesitated, the cup halfway to his mouth. He glanced at Will and asked, "Is there enough water so that Mr. Sample may have another cup?"

The water in the bucket was getting low. "Not now," Will answered. "Not until everyone has had some. Then I'll fill the bucket again."

"I can wait," Mansfield said. With a smile and a short bow he handed his cup of water to Jake, who drank noisily and greedily.

"I saw some dry, clean straw against the wall,

Jake," Mansfield said. "Come with me. I'll make a comfortable resting place for you."

Mills Mansfield is a good man, Will thought. *But how can he be both a good man and a forger?*

As Mansfield returned the cup to Will, another prisoner pushed forward. Will leaned around him to talk to Mansfield and said, "I'll soon bring more water."

Mansfield gave Will the same smile and bow he had given Jake. "Thank you, sir," he answered.

Will quickly kept his promise. After all the prisoners had drunk, he filled the bucket and carried it again to the passage. He dipped the cup into the water and handed it to Mansfield.

Unlike the other prisoners, Mansfield paused before reaching for the cup and again said, "Thank you."

Will waited, confused about the man's actions and appearance. For the crime of forgery Mansfield could be condemned to death. The General Court, at which all the prisoners would come to trial, would meet in only a few weeks. But Mills didn't seem to be afraid of his rapidly approaching death. Instead, he had combed his hair, had brushed the straw from his clothes, and appeared to be in a good humor.

"You are studying me so intently, you must have a question to ask," Mansfield said to Will, who realized he'd been staring.

"I—I . . . I wondered how . . . ," Will stammered, not knowing how to continue.

"How I ended up in the public gaol?" Mansfield winked at Will as he finished the boy's question. "As a matter of fact, I should not be here. What I did was not a crime."

"But forgery *is* a crime," Will burst out, speaking before he thought.

"Ah! Then you know why I was charged. But you do not know that the charge was unjustifiable. My employer agreed to pay me a certain sum for the work I did in selling his merchandise. However, when it came time for him to pay, he gave me only half of my rightful due. I simply forged his name on a promissory note which covered the rest of the amount. I ask you, sir, was that not right and fair?"

"My name is Will, Mr. Mansfield," Will said. "And you may have done what you thought was right and fair, but it wasn't within the law."

Mills thought a moment. "Hmmm, Will," he said. "If an intelligent lad like you thinks me guilty, then I suppose the court will be of the same mind."

"What does that mean?" Will asked.

Mills shrugged. "It means I am likely to be hanged."

Will expected Mansfield to look worried, even

fearful, but he smiled again and said, "Of course, since this is the first serious crime I've ever been accused of, I could plead benefit of clergy if I'm convicted. Do you know what that means?"

"No," Will said. "I don't."

"That means the court will not give me the death sentence. Instead, there in open court the heel of my right thumb will be branded."

Will winced and clutched the heel of his own right thumb as he imagined the awful pain of being burned with a branding iron and having that terrible mark for the rest of his life. But the prospect of the branding didn't seem to worry Mansfield. *Why not?* Will wondered.

"Thank you again for the water," Mansfield said. He walked to the back of the cell, where he pushed straw together into a bundle and sat down on it.

As Will left the passage he thought about Mansfield. Forger or not, Will couldn't help liking him.

Will then woke up his brother John and carried his chamber pot out to empty it. After the pot had been emptied, washed, and returned to its place under the bed, Will scrubbed his hands and face, combed his hair, and hurried to the hall, where a morning fire was blazing in the fireplace, to join his family for breakfast.

Plump, rosy-cheeked, and smiling, Mrs. Pelham

greeted each child with a hug. Then Mr. Pelham led the family in morning prayers. As soon as he had finished, Nellie brought in bowls of hominy and slices of ham, browned on the gridiron until their frizzled edges curled.

"Papa," Will said, remembering too late he was not supposed to speak with his mouth full, "what do you know about Mr. Mills Mansfield?"

Mrs. Pelham threw Will a quick look of caution. "Swallow every bit of that before you speak," she said.

Will's older sister, Sarah, turned to their mother. "Mama, quilted petticoats are the latest in fashion. Mary Geddy has one in pale blue. Just think how I would look in a soft green—to match my eyes."

"I want a petticoat, too," Elizabeth insisted. "And one for my doll."

Mrs. Pelham sighed. "Sarah, do you know how much time it would take to quilt a petticoat? As you can see, I have never been busier."

"Papa," Will repeated, this time making sure there was not a crumb of food in his mouth, "tell me about Mr. Mansfield."

"Mama, *I* will quilt the petticoat," Sarah interrupted.

Just then three-year-old Henry's cup of milk overturned on the table, and he began to wail. "John pushed me!"

"Did not!" John insisted.

Henry cried even more loudly.

"I scarce touched him with my elbow," John protested.

As Nellie hurried to wipe up the milk, Mrs. Pelham pulled Henry into her lap and soothed him. "Thankfully, we have more milk, sweet love. Do not cry. Nellie will bring you another cup."

"Please, Mama?" Sarah asked.

"Me too!" Elizabeth said.

"I didn't push him, Mama," John shouted.

"Did too!" Henry yelled.

Will shoved back his chair and walked to where his father was seated. "Papa," he said, raising his voice over the hubbub in the room, "I want to know about Mills Mansfield."

With a bite of ham halfway to his mouth, Mr. Pelham stopped. In surprise, he answered, "I told you Mansfield has been accused of forgery."

"But only because his employer wouldn't pay him."

"I hope you are not asking if the end justifies the means. You have been taught that this is not true."

Will sighed. "Papa, I only want to find out something about Mr. Mansfield. He seems to be a kind man, and in spite of what awaits him in court, he is in a good humor and treats others well."

"A forger is an untrustworthy person," Mr. Pelham answered. "Never allow an outward expression of pleasantness and warmth to blind you to hidden evil."

Mr. Pelham popped the ham into his mouth, so Will knew their conversation about Mr. Mansfield had come to an end. As he walked back to his place at the table, he shrugged off his father's warning. How could he think of Mr. Mansfield as evil, even though there was no doubt he had committed a crime? Will liked Mills Mansfield. No matter what Papa said, he was curious about Mr. Mansfield and determined to find out more about him.

Chapter Three

Will's father left the house soon after breakfast, hurrying so that he wouldn't be late for his appointment to teach the harpsichord to three sisters in a family that could well afford the lessons. Will knew that when his father returned, just before noon, he'd open the cell doors that led into the courtyard of the gaol, so that the prisoners could have some fresh air and sunlight. While his father was away, Will rushed through his chores and his studies, hoping he would have an opportunity to visit the prisoners afterward.

He read his lessons well, and his mother was pleased, but in his haste to write the answers to questions she asked, he carelessly neglected the point of his quill pen and spattered ink across his paper.

"Take a fresh sheet of paper and begin again," Mrs. Pelham told him.

Will groaned. "Mama, I have much to do. Pray excuse me," he begged.

John held up his paper. "Mama, see how neat my writing is."

" 'Tis very nice," Mrs. Pelham said.

John grinned and kicked Will's ankle under the table.

Again Mrs. Pelham looked at Will. "Pray tell me," she said. "What is it you must do that can't be done later?"

Will had no answer. He sighed and slumped in his chair.

Mrs. Pelham put an arm around Will's shoulders. " 'Tis easy to see that nothing good will come of making you sit in that chair this morning, child. You may be excused."

As Will jumped up, John cried, "Pray excuse me, too, Mama."

Mrs. Pelham shook her head. "Only one unruly student at a time, young man. Stay with your work."

Good, Will thought. John would have followed him to discover what he was up to. Will didn't want any tales brought back to Mama or Papa.

Will hurried down the passage to the door of the men's cell. As he arrived and looked through the bars, he saw Mansfield nearby, speaking with the slave, Emmanuel.

Mansfield didn't look surprised to see Will. He simply bowed his head politely and asked, "Will, has there been any word from Emmanuel's master?"

"Not that I know of," Will answered. "Emmanuel hasn't told us his master's name, and since the notice in *The Virginia Gazette* was so recently posted, no one has yet answered. Is it now Emmanuel's wish to return to his master?"

Mansfield's laugh was short and sharp. "On the contrary," he said. "His owner was cruel and beat him for no reason."

"If Emmanuel was planning to run away, why did he come to Williamsburg, where he could easily be found?" Will asked.

Mansfield put an arm around Emmanuel's shoulders, moving him toward the bars. "Why do we talk about Emmanuel as if he cannot speak for himself? Ask him your questions, Will, not me."

Blushing with embarrassment because Mansfield was right, Will looked directly at Emmanuel. His shirt had been torn, exposing dark welts across his upper arms, shoulders, and back. "I can see that your owner beat you, Emmanuel," Will said quietly. "Was it his nature to be angry?"

" 'Twas more than anger," Emmanuel said, his

28

voice low and his eyes downcast. "There was a terrible hatred in his beatin's. The last one near killed me. I crawled through the hedgerows that night to . . . to a place where I knew I'd be cared for. They told me that for a long time I lay close to death. It took me many weeks to recover."

"But he is your master," Will said, "and you were his property, bought and paid for. It was not right for you to run away."

"Think about it, Will," Mansfield answered. "Would you not run if it would save your life?"

Will shrugged. "But the law . . . ," he began. Confused, he was unable to finish what he had planned to say.

Mansfield smiled and clapped Emmanuel on the shoulder. "Be of good heart," he told him. "You said your owner cannot read. Therefore, he is unlikely to see the printed notice. Since—as you say—he has few friends, 'tis possible that no one will bring the notice to his attention. I do not know what will happen to you if he does not arrive to claim you within a reasonable time." Mansfield turned to Will. "As the gaoler's son, Will, do you know?"

Will nodded sadly. "If Emmanuel is not claimed, he will be forced to wear an iron collar around his neck and be hired out to pay for his expenses while in gaol."

In the silence that followed, Will could hear Emmanuel's heavy breathing. "I will not accept this willingly," he said. "I am a man. I do not deserve to be treated badly for wrongs I did not do."

"Nor do I," Mansfield said with a hearty chuckle. "So we will ease our troubles of the moment by hoping for a brighter future for both of us."

Will looked at Mansfield in surprise. How could he hope for a brighter future? He faced a painful branding, if he was fortunate enough to escape the usual death sentence for the crime of forgery. Neither event was a hopeful one. Will shuddered.

"Come now, Will," Mansfield said. "We need no long faces here. The cell is gloomy enough." He beckoned to Jake Sample, who was curled on a nearby pile of straw. "Mr. Sample is a fine teller of tales. Let us ask him to tell us a story."

As Jake hobbled within hearing distance, Mansfield winked at Will and said loudly, "I understand that last night Mr. Sample told you about the ghost of Blackbeard, who visits this gaol. He told me the story as well, and his tale was so fearful I could not sleep most of the night."

Jake grinned in delight, and Will gave a sigh of relief. If others were frightened by old Jake's story, then he had no reason to feel foolish.

Mansfield threw out his chest, held his arms akimbo, and stumped up and down the cell. In a deep voice he said, "I am the great Blackbeard, the fiercest pirate ever known, and I claim this stinking cell as my kingdom."

Will burst out laughing. Even Emmanuel had to smile. Jake nodded and chuckled. "That's the way Blackbeard talks, all right," Jake said. "He's used to getting his own way."

"No doubt about it," Mansfield said.

In a sneering voice, Colin Campbell asked, "Old man, why does this pirate speak only to you? None of the rest of us have heard him."

For a moment Jake seemed confused. Then he tried to explain. "Some of you snore loudly, so I do not sleep. I rarely sleep, so I listen. Blackbeard speaks to others, too. This cell is small, and I hear what he says. I talk to him. He talks to me. But not just to me. To others also."

Mr. Campbell laughed rudely. " 'Tis more likely it's you doing all the talking—and to yourself."

"Not I," Jake answered.

"Then tell us, what does this pirate ghost look like? Does he wear a plume in his hat? And a brace of pistols in his belt?"

Jake looked warily from side to side, then leaned forward, lowering his voice. "I have not seen him," he confided. "He hovers in the dark corners of the cell where the moonlight that streams through the barred window cannot enter."

"You're afraid of ghosts, old man," Mr. Campbell said. He laughed again, and two of the other prisoners joined in.

"Not I," Jake said. "I've met up with ghosts before and stood my ground."

"What ghosts?" Will blurted out before he thought.

One of the prisoners groaned. "Not another story," he complained.

Jake ignored him and said directly to Will, "It was on a winter's night, with the coldest wind that had ever been felt in these parts. As it howled around the corners of my house, I knew I would not dare to step outside.

"Suddenly there came a hard, loud knocking on my door. A tall figure, closely wrapped in a cloak and hood, stood on my doorstep. My visitor did not speak. He did not need to. I hurried to let him inside, offering him a chair by the fire." Jake lowered his voice and said mysteriously, "But strange to say, he kept his hood up and his cloak wrapped around his body. Instead of taking the chair I offered, he chose one in a dark corner of the room.

" 'Will you have something to eat or drink?' I asked him, but the stranger only shook his head. He still did not speak.

"At first I was puzzled. He had no wish to eat or drink or to be seated by the warmth of the fire? I tried to look into his eyes, but I saw only darkness under the hood of his cloak. It was then I became certain that my visitor was a ghostly presence."

Someone chuckled, but Will was intent on the story. "What did you do?" he asked.

"I rose to my feet and pointed at the closed door. 'Leave my home,' I told the stranger. 'There is not room in this dwelling for both of us. One of us will have to go, and it will not be me.'

"He stood, and without a word he walked to the door, opened it, and stepped outside. I quickly locked the door behind him and never saw or heard from him again."

"You're telling us you chased a ghost away?" Mr. Campbell said with a laugh.

"Aye. He was none other," Jake answered. "And if the ghost returned, I'd do it again."

Everyone laughed, including Jake himself.

"You sent some poor, freezing spirit into the worst wind that had ever been?" Mr. Campbell taunted.

Jake frowned. "I said it was the coldest wind, but I did not say it was the *worstest* wind I've ever known. The worstest wind came when I was but a lad. It blew in from the ocean with a torrent of rain. It pulled trees from the land by their roots and tossed horses and cows about as if they were no heavier than puffs of smoke. It even blew fish right out of the river onto the banks. I filled three bushel baskets with fish. There was enough to feed my family and the neighbors for weeks to come."

Mr. Mansfield grinned and winked at Will. "Jake has a fine talent for spinning stories," he said.

Will nodded. "Tell us more," he said, forgetting whatever other chores awaited him.

Will decided that Jake's story about Blackbeard was the best of all he had heard, and he looked forward to repeating it to his friend Joseph Hay and to Joseph's cousin Robert Greenhow. Between his chores and the studies his mother assigned him, there wasn't much time left to spend with friends, but one early evening near the end of the week Will, Joseph, and Robert met on the green next to Joseph's house. Robert was only ten—a plump, serious, always hungry tagalong—but he was readily accepted by Will and Joseph. Robert's father owned a store, so Robert could be counted on to bring sugar candy.

Will found that Robert was also a good audience. While Joseph—a year older than Will—scoffed at Jake's tale, Robert listened with wide eyes.

"Blackbeard, huh!" Joseph said with a laugh. As he pushed his cocked hat to the back of his head, stray wisps of blond hair fell across his forehead. "Why does his ghost prowl the cells? Being a ghost, he could go anywhere. He could choose a comfortable chair by the fire, or—" Joseph lowered his voice, ducked his head, and began to inch toward Will. "Or he could creep up the stairs, slide under the door of your bedchamber, pull his sword, and run you through!"

As Robert let out a startled yelp, Joseph flung himself on Will. Laughing, they rolled over and over on the grass.

Will and Joseph finally sat up, retrieving their hats and brushing grass from their clothing. Robert stared at them solemnly and with a wavering voice said, "He could, you know."

"He could what?" Will asked.

"Go into your room, right through the walls. He's a ghost, isn't he?"

Joseph bent over laughing. Will tried to laugh, too, but he could picture old Blackbeard hovering over his bed, sword raised. Wishing that Joseph hadn't brought up the idea, he scoffed, "Nobody believes in ghosts."

"Yes, they do," Robert insisted. "A widow woman who lives in Richmond one night woke up and in the moonlight saw her dead husband plain as day. He stared at her with big, dark, hollow eyes and pointed at the floor in the corner of the room. The next morning she pulled up the loose floorboards and found a box filled with pieces of eight. She used the money to marry again and move to North Carolina."

As usual, Joseph scoffed, but he asked, "Who told you that?"

"My father did," Robert said. "One of his customers told him."

"I don't believe it."

"Neither do I," Will said, loyal to Joseph, but his heart beat a little faster, and he had to fight the desire to look behind him to see who or what might be lurking in the shadows.

Mrs. Elizabeth Hay stepped out on her porch and called, "Joseph, it's time to come in. It's growing late."

Will waved to Mrs. Hay, who smiled and waved in return before she went back inside.

"Can you come again tomorrow?" Joseph asked Will.

"*I* can," Robert said.

Will shrugged. "I don't know," he answered. "Papa finds much for me to do, and Mama adds to it. Taking care of the prisoners along with my chores and study is a lot of work."

Robert nodded. "I'm glad I don't live in the public gaol—especially since it's haunted by a ghost."

Will gulped. "That isn't funny, Robert."

"I'm not trying to be funny," Robert said. He tilted his head, studying Will. "If Blackbeard does go into your bedchamber in the night, how will we find out?"

"Will is sure to tell us," Joseph said, and snickered.

"I don't think he could," Robert said. "I heard that a lad in Norfolk saw a ghost, and he was so frightened his hair became white and he turned into a wrinkled old man who could only mutter gibberish till the day he died."

Will bent almost nose to nose with Robert and said, "I don't want to hear one more word about ghosts. If I do I'll . . . I'll . . . tell Blackbeard how to find your house and send him to see you."

Robert's eyes opened wide. "It's getting dark. I have to go home," he said. He turned and ran.

"That goes for you, too," Will said to Joseph, and laughed.

"I don't mind if Blackbeard's ghost comes to visit me," Joseph said. "I'll ask him where he hid his treasure. I'll share it with you, and then we'll both be rich."

Will sighed. "Rich enough, I hope, for Papa to leave his occupation as gaoler and our family to live in a house that's inhabited by neither ghosts nor criminals."

Chapter Four

Will hurried home to avoid being late for his chores. "There you are, child," Mrs. Pelham said as he entered the house. "Nellie has cooked the food for the prisoners. You can take it to them now."

Will carried to the cells the bowls of hominy topped with thin pieces of meat that were mostly fat and gristle. He wished his father could give the prisoners something better to eat, but the budget for food was small. Will sniffed the meat and made a face. No doubt these were scraps donated, at Papa's urging, by one of the taverns.

Will had no time to talk to the prisoners. Papa was to play the harpsichord at the theater where the plays began at seven o'clock.

Will thought with pleasure of the evening ahead.

He'd be sitting with his father, turning the pages of his music, letting the music swell through the play-house until it wrapped around him, lifting him through the candlelit dusk into a warm, snug cocoon of beauty. He loved hearing his father play, as did all the people of Williamsburg.

As he entered the hall, Will ran to his father. "Papa," he said, "will some of the burgesses be at the theater?"

"I expect some of them to attend." Mr. Pelham smiled. "I have played before them and have even played music with them."

Will was interested. "Whom have you played with, Papa?"

"Before young Thomas Jefferson was a burgess, while he was studying law under George Wythe, he purchased a fine violin and hired me to accompany him," Mr. Pelham said. "It was a most pleasurable evening."

Mrs. Pelham came into the room, smoothing her petticoats. "You talked of Thomas Jefferson. What has that outspoken young man done now?"

"Madam," Mr. Pelham said patiently, "pray remember that Mr. Jefferson is a highly respected member of the House of Burgesses."

Mrs. Pelham's eyes sparked with indignation. "Perhaps so, but I seem to remember talk that two

39

years ago, after being newly elected to the House of Burgesses, Mr. Jefferson made known that he favors the emancipation of slaves. I ask you, what would I do without Toby and Nellie to help me with all the work that must be done around this house and gaol? What would any of the women in Virginia do?"

"Do not fret yourself," Mr. Pelham told her. " 'Twas only talk. Toby and Nellie are still here, as you wish them to be."

As Mrs. Pelham swept back into the bedchamber, Will asked, "Father, Mr. Jefferson owns slaves, does he not?"

"Indeed he does," Mr. Pelham answered.

"Mama said he spoke against slavery. Then why does he not free his own slaves?"

Mr. Pelham frowned as he thought. "Whether right or wrong, freeing one's slaves is not an action a man can take alone. We have purchased slaves. They are our property. And they're necessary to our comforts in life. You heard what your mother said. How would she keep up the household without the help of Toby and Nellie?

"The loss of slaves would also mean the loss of income for many businessmen and plantation owners. Mr. Jefferson could not bear this burden alone. Do you understand, Will?"

"I think so, Papa," Will answered, but he was still

puzzled. Either an issue was right or it was wrong. And if a man thought something he was doing was wrong, then how could he proceed as if it were right?

Mr. Pelham clapped his hands on Will's shoulders, interrupting his thoughts. "Son," he said, "I'm afraid I have bad news. I know how much you enjoy the plays, but I must ask you to forgo tonight's performance. I was unable to hire someone to be in charge of the prisoners tonight while I am away from the gaol. Will you stand in for me?"

Will took a step back. "Papa! You want me to stay with the prisoners and miss your playing?"

"Yes, Will. I am sorry, but I need your help."

"Can't you put Toby in charge?" Will pleaded.

"Toby is a slave," Mr. Pelham said quietly. " 'Twould be amiss to leave him alone in the gaol where he could have free access to the cells."

Startled, Will asked, "Do you not trust Toby? He has never disobeyed you."

Mr. Pelham's brow wrinkled, and he looked unhappy. "It is not a matter of trusting Toby. I have no choice," he said. "I accepted the duties of a gaoler, and I must perform them in a way that will satisfy the councillors. That means I—and no one else—am responsible for those keys."

"Then I shouldn't have the keys either," Will reasoned, still unwilling to miss the play.

"You are my son. Your presence would be acceptable. I will entrust you with the keys to use if any unforeseen difficulty should arise."

Will hated to give up the argument. "What unforeseen difficulty?" he demanded.

"An unforeseen difficulty is one we have not expected. Therefore, I am unable to answer your question, which was unforeseen in itself." Mr. Pelham's lips curled in a teasing smile, and Will couldn't help smiling, too.

"Tell me what to do, Papa," he said.

"Just be aware of the prisoners' needs," Mr. Pelham said. "Because it will soon be dark, most of them will sleep. But one of them may need water, or perhaps medication for the itch that comes from the bugs in the straw. Mr. Campbell has lately complained of a stomachache. Nellie knows the proper medication and will help you."

No more was said about Will's duties because Mrs. Pelham called the family to be seated for supper.

In no time at all the family had eaten. Will's mother and the younger children retired for the night, and Mr. Pelham left, taking Sarah with him to turn the pages of the music. The house became quiet. Except for Nellie and Toby in the basement kitchen, Will alone was awake, the ring of keys in his possession.

42

For a short while he sat and read by the fire, but soon the light grew too dim. Carrying his candle, he walked down the passage to the cells. The women's cell was silent, so Will tiptoed to the barred window in the men's cell door. He could hear snoring and an occasional moan, but he jumped as a loud "Hssst!" sounded in his ears.

"Mr. Sample?" Will asked.

"Right. 'Tis me," Jake answered. "Come closer, lad. I have something to tell you."

Will stepped close to the bars. Unwilling to wake the other prisoners, he kept his voice low. "What do you need, Mr. Sample?"

" 'Tis not me what needs. 'Tis Blackbeard. He talks to me, as you well know. And sometimes he talks to others and even though he whispers I can't help but overhear." Jake lowered his voice and said, "He speaks of leaving this loathsome place."

"Good. I hope he does. You can tell me about it in the morning," Will answered. He took a step backward. He had no wish to hear Jake's imaginary tales about Blackbeard in the gloom of the dark passage. "Good night, Mr. Sample," he whispered, and ran back to the hall and the warmth of the fire.

As he put the candle down on the table, he saw by the clock on the corner cabinet that his father and Sarah would not return for close to an hour. It was too dark to read, and there was no one to talk to. Will sighed, wondering what he could do to keep the time from moving so slowly.

As he heard voices coming from the open doorway to the basement stairs, he perked up. That was the answer. He could visit with Nellie and Toby. When he was younger—even younger than John—they had told him about the land from which their parents came, across the sea. Surely they had more stories to share.

Will started down the stairs but paused as Toby's angry words carried loudly and clearly. "All I say is, no man should be treated as badly as Emmanuel was treated. He's afraid to go back. He's sure to be whipped to death."

Nellie's voice was sad. "Why, oh why, did Emmanuel come this way instead of going west to freedom? Didn't he know someone might recognize him?"

"He told me he'd heard about the dangers of Indian territory and the wild animals that prowl the mountains and valleys. He was afraid. He'd also heard there were some freed slaves living in Williamsburg. He hoped to be taken for a freedman."

Will gave a start. Emmanuel had *told* Toby? Will had heard his father warn Toby that slaves were not allowed contact with the prisoners. That was the reason Will instead of Toby brought them their water and food.

Will was shocked that Toby had broken the rule. What would his father do when he found out? Then Will thought of poor Emmanuel, terrified that his owner would come for him. If Toby's friendship could give Emmanuel some comfort, Will decided, he would keep the information to himself. Breaking this small rule could not harm his father.

"Huh!" Nellie grumbled to Toby. "It seems Emmanuel might have a better chance with the wild animals than with his owner, when he comes to claim him."

"If he comes in time," Toby answered quietly.

"What d'you mean, if he comes in time?" Nellie asked. "The notice was posted in the newspaper. I heard Mr. Pelham say so. The man will show up sooner or later, and Mr. Pelham will hold Emmanuel in the gaol or hire him out until he does."

Toby didn't answer immediately, and Nellie demanded, "Well? Won't he?"

Will, eager to hear the answer and what else might follow, sat on the stairs, which creaked as he shifted his weight.

There was a long silence; then Toby said loudly, "I don't know nothin' about Emmanuel's owner or what Mr. Pelham will do. Slaves don't talk to the prisoners."

He said that for me, Will thought. *He knows I'm here.*

As silently as possible, Will got to his feet and walked back into the hall, where he sat again in the chair by the fireplace. He wondered what Toby had been intending to say about Emmanuel's owner. Perhaps he had planned to tell Nellie something about Emmanuel. Whatever it was, Will had lost his chance to find out.

Later, when his father returned with Sarah, he asked Will, "Did you have any trouble while I was away?"

"None, Papa," Will answered. He wished Sarah a good night and watched her leave the hall before he added, "Jake wanted to tell me another ghost story. Except for that, all was peaceful."

"I am thankful for your help, son," Mr. Pelham said. "I see that your mother has not waited up for me. Caring for the family tires her out these days."

Surprised, Will asked, "But why? It never used to." Then the answer came to him. "Will there be another baby, Papa?"

"In the early spring," Mr. Pelham answered. For just an instant his eyes clouded with sorrow, and he said, "I pray that this child will be born healthy and will thrive. Your mother and I will always mourn your brothers and sisters who died while still very young."

Since these children were remembered in the family's prayers, Will knew there had been six, and he knew each of their names. But with the exception of Mary, who had been born when Will was seven and had died the following year, they were strangers to him. Will, too, hoped that this baby, who would be his parents' fourteenth child, would be healthy.

"Hurry along to bed, Will. Sleep well," Mr. Pelham said.

"Good night, Papa," Will answered.

Will turned toward the passage, then stopped as his father said, "Tomorrow will be a busy day in Williamsburg because Virginia's new governor, John Murray, fourth Earl of Dunmore, will arrive in the afternoon from London. I hope you will take time to join the crowds who will give Lord Dunmore a proper welcome to our colony."

Will was curious about the new governor who would replace the acting governor, William Nelson, president of the Council. He quickly answered, "I'll take Joseph. We'll go together."

Mr. Pelham smiled. "Fine. Now, I have another

suggestion for you. On Friday afternoon, let us make time to visit the church together. You are coming along well with your lessons on the harpsichord. If you are interested, I would like to begin teaching you to play the organ."

Although Will loved to listen to his father play, he had no wish for music lessons of his own. But his heart leapt with excitement at the prospect of spending time alone with his father. "Perhaps I could come with you just to hear you practice, Papa," he said. "I could never learn to play as well as you do."

"Yes, you can," Mr. Pelham said, "if you practice often."

Practice often? When would I find any time to practice? Will thought. But at least the lessons would allow him to share time with his father, and that pleased him.

After Will wished his father a good night, he walked silently and cautiously down the passage and up the stairs to the bedchamber. Although he tensed as he passed the cells, waiting for Jake's whisper to pierce the silence, the only sounds were the murmurs from the men who were sleeping.

When Will reached the bedchamber, John mumbled in his sleep. Will gently tucked the bedding around his brother's small shoulders and kissed his forehead. Will loved his brothers and sisters, and he thought about the new baby to come. The baby would be welcome, but . . .

Will sighed. With another mouth to feed, it would be even more important for his father to keep both his occupations. Even if the ghost of Blackbeard should turn up with a treasure chest filled with pieces of eight—as Joseph wished—it would not be enough to allow Papa to quit his position as gaoler. Will was afraid that the public gaol would be the Pelhams' home for a long while to come.

Chapter Five

The next afternoon Will, Joseph, and Robert ran to the Palace Green, outside the governor's palace, to catch a glimpse of Lord Dunmore. There were more people on hand than Will had expected, and it was impossible to edge through the tightly packed crowd to reach a place from which they could see the governor.

"I can hear the carriages, but I can't see them," Joseph complained.

"Ouch!" Robert cried out. "Someone stepped on my foot!"

"Perhaps we could move to the side," Will suggested.

"There's no room at the side," Joseph answered.

"I think we should leave before we are trampled to

death," Robert said. "I heard about a man who was trampled to death. His tongue lay on the ground and his eyeballs shot from his head and—"

" 'Tis time we left." Will grabbed Joseph's arm. Tugging and elbowing, he managed to work his way out of the crowd, pulling Joseph with him. Robert, who had clung to Joseph, popped out of the crowd like a cork from a bottle.

"I wonder what the new governor looks like," Joseph said.

"I wonder what his carriage looks like," Robert said. Will's thoughts, however, weren't on Governor Dunmore. He was busy worrying about the music lesson he was to have with his father the next day. As much as Will loved listening to music, especially the beautiful concerts his father played at Bruton Parish Church, he did not enjoy studying music himself, and he had no real talent for it, either. But Will's father was so busy with his various jobs that the music lessons were the only way for Will to have Mr. Pelham to himself for a little while. And it would break his father's heart to find out that Will didn't share his love or his talent for playing music. What was he going to do the next day, when the awful truth was sure to come out?

Suddenly Joseph's voice burst into Will's thoughts. "Race you to Nicholson Street!" he shouted. Joseph took off at a run, with Robert and Will close behind him and racing to catch up.

On Friday afternoon, Will's father kept his promise, escorting him to Bruton Parish Church for his first lesson on the organ. It was not a private time for father and son, as Will had wished, because the prisoner John Watts had to be brought along to pump the bellows of the organ.

And Will was not free to chat with his father. Instead, he had to concentrate on treble and bass notes and stops and rests and all that he must learn and remember. His first attempts at playing a chord made him wince. Learning the harpsichord had been much easier.

Will glanced down from the organ loft. Two women—probably having heard the music Mr. Pelham had played as he showed Will what to do—had entered the open door of the church. But, hearing Will's attempts, they turned and quickly scurried out again.

"Papa, the sounds I make are not like your music," Will complained.

Mr. Pelham smiled. "When I first began to learn music, do you not think my attempts sounded like yours? I made mistakes, but I tried again and again. I practiced. I studied. I learned. When Sarah first began her lessons on the organ, she made many mistakes, but she greatly improved with practice. If you love music more than anything else and wish someday to be an organist—"

"I love music," Will interrupted, "especially the way you play it. But it is not what I love most. What I love most of all is books. I like to visit the store in Mr. William Rind's shop, where he prints *The Virginia Gazette*. Although I do not buy his books, he is always happy to let me look at those he has for sale."

Mr. Pelham put an arm around Will's shoulders. Will expected to see disappointment on his father's face, but instead he saw what looked like a fleeting expression of relief. Perhaps Will's father, too, had wondered when he'd have time in his overly busy days to give Will lessons or where Will would find the many hours he'd need for practice.

"Your dreams may lead you to the printing of your own books someday," Mr. Pelham said. "Pray go downstairs and sit in one of the pews, son. Mr. Watts will pump the organ bellows, and I will play for you. Would you like a selection composed by Handel or Bach?"

"Handel," Will answered before he scurried down the stairs and settled into a seat near the altar.

The music began with notes so light they spiraled

down with the tiny motes in the sunlight that poured through the windows. But the music soon became more powerful, spilling from the church, so that passersby silently crept inside to listen, too.

Will closed his eyes, at peace with the music, with his father, and with a dream that someday might come true.

That evening Will and his father arrived home earlier than expected. As Will entered the passage that led to the stairs to his bedchamber, he passed Toby, hurrying out.

Toby's eyes were frightened, and Will felt certain he'd been at the cell door talking to Emmanuel, which was strictly forbidden.

But why was it forbidden? Surely there could be no harm in allowing Emmanuel a friend to talk to.

Mr. Pelham called from the hall, "Toby?"

Toby stiffened, a flicker of terror in his eyes.

Will shook his head and whispered, "I won't tell."

Toby gave Will a cautious look, then hurried to answer Mr. Pelham.

Did Toby hear what I told him? Will wondered. *Did he know what I meant?*

Will felt a twinge of guilt, but he shrugged it off. He was not exactly keeping secrets from his father. And he couldn't be sure that Toby had even been talking to the prisoner. *If I find out anything for cer-*

tain, then I'll tell Papa. He consoled himself with that and headed off to bed.

During the next week, as hard as he tried, Will had little time to chat with Mansfield. During the few moments when he was able to visit the cell, old Jake pressed his face against the window bars, relating one of his imaginative tales.

One day he called Will over and told him in a hushed voice, "Blackbeard is going to join his men."

"That's good news," Will answered. "It's time for that ghost to leave."

Jake's whisper grew more insistent. "There's more. I may be old, but my hearing is good. I know what I overheard. When Blackbeard leaves, he will take someone with him."

Will was puzzled. "How could he? Ghosts can't do that."

"Oh, yes, they can," Jake said. "Ghosts like Blackbeard are used to getting their own way. They can do whatever they wish."

Will felt uncomfortable. He glanced around, hoping that no one was behind him. Then he couldn't help asking, "Who will Blackbeard take?"

"I don't know. Maybe *you!*" Jake said. His loud, rough cackle seemed to bounce off the walls.

Will shook his head impatiently. How could anyone think it was humorous to talk of ghosts? "There is no ghost of Blackbeard in the cell, Mr. Sample," Will grumbled. "Ghosts don't exist."

Mills Mansfield joined Jake at the barred window. He smiled broadly at Will. "Do not dismiss Mr. Sample's tales of Blackbeard. I assure you, ghosts *do* exist," he said. "Have you not heard others speak of ghosts?"

"Yes, I have," Will admitted. Remembering Robert Greenhow's tale, he reluctantly added, "There was a woman in Richmond who claimed she saw the ghost of her dead husband."

Emmanuel, who was standing just behind Mansfield, chuckled. "Once, in the deep of night, my master hollered out so loud everyone in the household was afeard. We all ran to help him. He was sittin' in bed, shakin' like a young tree in the wind. He kep' babblin' that he saw his first wife, dressed all in white. She frowned and pointed at him as she came closer and closer."

"What happened?" Will asked.

"Nothin'," Emmanuel said. "Which is sad. We hoped her ghost would give him what he deserved."

Jake, his own good humor restored, piped up. "I pay close attention to what Blackbeard says."

Mansfield clapped him on the shoulder as he winked and smiled at Will. "As well you should," he said.

Will, sorry that he'd been impatient with Jake, quickly said, "I like to hear your stories, Mr. Sample."

"Do you?" Jake said. "Oh, I have lots of tales to tell, because I've led a long and busy life. I haven't told you about the day Colonel George Washington and his troops traveled the road by my farm. It was a warm day, and I ran out to offer them cool water to drink."

Jake went on with the story, and Will—copying Mansfield—pretended to listen intently as though he had not heard it before. It befitted a man to be kind and thoughtful . . . like Mansfield.

Will still couldn't decide how he felt about Mansfield. He had broken the law. He was a forger. On the other hand, he was genteel in his dress and in his behavior. He had a pleasing nature and was always in good spirits. But he was a criminal, and he might soon be put to death. The jumble of facts was too difficult to sort out, so once again Will pushed them out of his mind.

It wasn't until after the evening meal that Will came face to face with Toby for the first time since Friday evening. "Good evening, Toby," he said.

Toby stopped, eyeing him warily. "Good evening, Master Will," Toby said. He held himself so tensely that a muscle in his neck throbbed.

Will was puzzled. He was certain that Toby was waiting for him to say something, but Will didn't know what to do or say that would put Toby at ease. He still wasn't sure that Toby had been talking to Emmanuel or any of the other prisoners. And even if he had been, Will wasn't quite sure what to do about it. After all, he sympathized with Emmanuel and could understand how having someone to talk to, like Toby, might give him some comfort. But if Mr. Pelham were to find out that Toby was communicating with one of the prisoners—an escaped slave, no less!—Toby would face a harsh punishment. Will would, too, if his father discovered that he'd been hiding the information.

Toby hesitated, then asked, "Did you want me for something, Master Will?"

"No, Toby. Continue to go about your work," Will said. "You are doing a good job."

For just a second Toby looked directly into Will's eyes. "I thank you for saying so, Master Will," he replied. Then he dropped his gaze once again and continued on his way.

Toby still seems disturbed. He doesn't trust me, Will thought. *What can I do to make him trust me?*

Will walked outside and sat on the front steps of the gaol. The evening was not too cool, and early stars were already dotting the clear, cloudless sky.

"Will!" came a shout.

He lifted his head and saw Joseph running toward

him, his cousin Robert at his heels. Will jumped up and dashed to meet them.

"Colonel Washington is at Raleigh Tavern," Joseph said. "Mr. Southall let us enter the back passage so we could see him."

"I used to hide in that passage and spy on the tavern's guests when my father owned it." Joseph looked sad for a moment as he remembered the days when his father had owned the tavern. After his father's death a year ago, Mr. Southall had taken it over.

"What was Colonel Washington doing at the tavern?" Will asked, hoping to distract his friend.

"He was doing what tavern visitors usually do— eating, drinking, talking with his friends," Robert answered.

Joseph smiled at Will. "I think you've been spending too much time at the gaol. You forget what real people do. Jake Sample must have filled your head with too many ghost stories."

Will gave a quick glance toward the gaol. "Jake Sample doesn't just talk about ghosts. He speaks of other things, too. He told me he gave Colonel Washington a drink of water and some advice about how to defeat the French by flanking their troops the way sheep are herded."

"He told a colonel how to win a battle?" Joseph began to laugh so hard, he had to hold his stomach.

Will laughed, too, then waited patiently until Joseph straightened, taking a deep breath and wiping his eyes. "That's even better than the Blackbeard story," Joseph managed to say.

"Blackbeard is still there," Will said, "but Jake has heard him say he will soon leave the public gaol."

Joseph grinned. "That's what you want, isn't it?"

"You haven't heard the rest. Blackbeard plans to take someone with him."

"Who?" Robert asked.

Will smiled and shrugged. "Jake said he didn't know. He said it could be me."

"Ghosts can't take people with them," Joseph scoffed.

"Oh, yes, they can," Robert said solemnly. "A man near the James River beat one of his slaves so badly he died. The slave came back as a ghost one night and just picked up that cruel man and carried him to the river and threw him in. He sank straight to the bottom and drowned."

"Where'd you hear that story?" Joseph asked.

"From Mrs. Geddy's kitchen slave. She heard it from someone whose brother saw it happen."

Joseph sighed. "If he saw it happen, why didn't he fish the cruel man out of the river and save his life?"

"Don't ask me," Robert said. "I just told you what I know about it."

Will smiled. "You mean the ghost of Blackbeard *could* take me with him? I don't believe so."

Joseph took two steps closer to Will, staring into his eyes. "He could. Oh, yes, he could," Joseph said. "I can see it all now. Blackbeard will float through the door to your bedchamber. He'll grab your shoulders, lifting you from your bed. You'll kick and scream, but no one will hear you. He'll carry you through the door . . . No, wait. You won't be a ghost . . . not yet. You can't float through a door, so Blackbeard will have to kick it open. You'll float down the passage and—"

"And you'll be there, ready to save my life." Will grabbed Joseph around the neck, and they fell to the ground, rolling, wrestling, and laughing.

As they finally lay quietly on the grass, Robert sat down cross-legged next to them. He poked Will in the shoulder. "The pirate Blackbeard was bad. He was a thief and a murderer," he said. "If he takes someone with him, it won't be to a very nice place. You had better find out."

Will sat up, staring at Robert. "Find out what?" Will asked.

Robert shook his head. "Not what—who. Find out *who* he plans to take with him. Remember what Jake Sample said. It could be *you.*"

Chapter Six

That evening at supper, Will thought again of his suspicions about Toby. Was his sympathy for Emmanuel causing him to make a wrong decision? By keeping silent, was he helping a poor, frightened slave and saving Toby from trouble? Or was he being disloyal to his father?

As Will watched Nellie set a plate of baked apples on the table and fill each person's bowl with leftover mutton stew, he thought again of his mother's distress at the idea of emancipating the slaves. Surely his mother had been right. It would be very difficult for her to manage the household and care for her family without the help his father had purchased for her.

Yet Emmanuel's owner had most certainly been wrong when he beat Emmanuel nearly to the point of death. As he tried to reason, Will's head began to hurt. Why could the facts involving right and wrong not be clearer? Why were they so muddled?

"Will, dear," his mother suddenly said, "you are frowning. Are you not well?"

"I'm well, Mother," Will said. He sat up straight as Nellie placed a steaming bowl of stew before him.

"When will you have your next lesson on the church organ?"

Will hesitated, wondering if his father would speak up.

But John interrupted. "*I* will have organ lessons, too, Mama. If Will has lessons, then I should have them."

"Me too!" Henry shouted. He began to hammer on the table with his spoon, but his hand hit his nearly full cup of milk and it tipped over.

Nellie ran to get a cloth with which to wipe up the milk, and Mrs. Pelham dabbed at a puddle on the edge of the table with her napkin.

"Mama!" Sarah complained. "Can't you make Henry stop spilling his milk?"

"Henry spilled it on purpose," John said.

"Did not!" Henry cried.

"Now, now, the little lad is only three," Mrs. Pelham said.

"Am not!" Henry screeched. As the others laughed, he realized his mistake and began to sob in anger.

Elizabeth smiled smugly as she shouted above the hubbub, "*I* didn't spill my milk when *I* was three."

"You did too," John said. "And what's more, you knocked an entire bowl of porridge into Mama's lap."

Elizabeth sniffled and her eyes welled with tears.

Mr. Pelham clapped his hands loudly. "Enough," he said.

The wailing and sniffling ceased as all the children looked at their father.

"I have recently purchased a small volume titled the *School of Manners, Or Rules for Children's Behavior.* There is a chapter which covers behavior at the table. If your mother and I have to deal with one more instance of misbehavior, we will spend some time at the table reading the rules. Do you all understand?"

"Yes, Papa," John said. "Pay attention, Elizabeth."

Elizabeth's cheeks turned pink. "I'm not the one who causes trouble. It's Henry," she complained.

"I do not!" Henry shouted.

"Papa, I have many things to do," Sarah begged. "Surely you can't mean I would have to stay and listen to the rules, too."

"I said we will *all* stay for the reading," Mr. Pelham replied. "And we will do it today, children, if you do not tend to your manners."

There was immediate silence. Mrs. Pelham smiled reassuringly at the children, then said to her husband, "Of what were we speaking?"

Mr. Pelham buttered a piece of bread. "I have not the slightest idea," he answered.

Will was glad. Now was not the time to explain to his mother that he wasn't having any more lessons on the church organ. He had so much else to think about. Sooner or later his father would remember to tell her. That would be the best way.

Will began to eat his stew. He had just taken a large mouthful when John suddenly said, "Papa, I couldn't hear what Toby said, but I think he was talking to the prisoners today."

"No!" Will cried out. "You heard him talking to me." To Will's dismay, a small piece of potato shot from his mouth to the table and a line of gravy dribbled down his chin.

He quickly wiped his face with his napkin, then chewed and swallowed his food as fast as possible. But his mother gave him a disapproving look and said, "Child, you have been told over and over again not to speak with your mouth full."

Mr. Pelham shoved back his chair and rose. "Each of you stay in your place," he said. "I shall get that *School of Manners* book of which I spoke."

Sarah glared at Will, but John grinned gleefully

and whispered, "Will's the one in trouble. I thought it would be Henry."

Mr. Pelham seated himself again, the small volume in his hands.

"You would do well to pay close attention, Will," Mrs. Pelham said. "Colonel George Washington is an example of a perfect gentleman who surely would have studied rules similar to these and taken them to heart. Perhaps you should follow his good example."

Mr. Pelham cleared his throat, then began to read, " 'Spit not, cough not, nor blow thy nose at table if it may be avoided; but if there be necessity, do it aside, and without much noise.' "

"Papa, I didn't—"

"You have not broken *all* the rules in this list," Mr. Pelham told Will, "but you will certainly benefit by learning and following them." He raised the book and began to read again. " 'Foul not the tablecloth. Gnaw not Bones at the Table, but clean them with thy knife (unless they be very small ones) and hold them not with a whole hand, but with two fingers.' "

Resigned, Will listened obediently. It was boring to have to hear a long list of rules, but it was his fault for trying to talk with his mouth full. At least it kept Papa from questioning John about Toby. If Will knew his father, after he'd finished this lesson, any discussion about Toby would be well out of his mind.

Mr. Pelham paused, then read slowly and firmly, " 'Stuff not thy mouth so as to fill thy cheeks; be content with smaller mouthfuls.' "

Will, his face burning with embarrassment, nodded. "I'll remember, Papa," he said.

Turning a page, Mr. Pelham said, "Ah, 'Rules for Behavior in Discourse.' Rule number one, 'Among superiors speak not till thou art asked.' "

"Papa," Sarah asked in a small, unhappy voice, "have we not heard enough rules for tonight?"

Mr. Pelham closed the book. "There are many other lessons worthy to be learned," he said.

"Don't read any more, Papa," Elizabeth said, her eyes wide and solemn. "We'll be good."

Mr. Pelham looked at Will. "Did you gain from the reading, son?"

"Yes, Papa," Will said. He squirmed uncomfortably in his chair. He hoped his father wouldn't ask questions. He'd heard much of what had been read, but not all of it, because he couldn't get his mind off Toby.

He had made his decision. He would try to catch Toby alone so that he could talk to him. He'd have to warn Toby to be more careful. If John had heard Toby talking with Emmanuel, others in the family might hear him, too. Toby could find himself in great trouble.

Later, Will helped tuck John into bed, then blew out the candle. Across the large room Sarah was already asleep. Will could hear her steady breathing.

Still dressed, with only his shoes and stockings removed, he lay on top of his bed waiting for the house to become silent. Toby, who had to bank the fire in the hall, and Nellie, who had to finish her work in the kitchen, would be the last to retire.

Impatiently Will waited until he heard sounds below that told him his parents had entered their bedchamber, where Henry and Elizabeth would have been tucked into their trundle beds and were sure to be asleep.

Barefoot, without candlelight to guide him, Will crept down the stairs, then through the passage. A low moaning came from the men's cell, and Will hurried past, shivering. The hall was dark, but the door to the basement stairs was open, and candlelight shone from the kitchen. Will could hear the murmur of voices as Toby and Nellie spoke to each other.

Cautiously, quietly, so that his father wouldn't hear him, Will began to descend the stairs.

He had reached the sixth stair when he heard Toby say, ". . . where to go when a man escapes."

Will stopped short, clutching the stair rail. *Escapes?*

Nellie's voice was scornful. "Don't be foolish, Toby, with your talk about escapes. What if somebody hears you?"

Will flattened himself against the wall, scarcely daring to breathe.

"I was only sayin' what *might* be," Toby grumbled.

"Don't be talkin' about it at all," Nellie said. "Hurry up. Go upstairs and bank the fire. It's time to be goin' to bed."

"Listen to me, Nellie," Toby began. "Why should a slave be considered less than a man? And why should anybody have the right to rob another man of his freedom and make him a slave?"

"Don't trouble me with your questions," Nellie said. "There are no answers. That's just the way things are."

Will didn't stay to hear another word. As silently and quickly as he could, he ran up the stairs, through the dark hall, and down the passage. He didn't stop until he reached his bedchamber. Pulling off his breeches, he dived into bed, tucking the bedding under his chin and rubbing his cold toes up and down his legs to warm them.

Nellie and Toby hadn't seen or heard him. He was sure of that. And Toby hadn't spoken of a real escape. He had said only "what might be." So why was Will still afraid of what might happen?

Chapter Seven

Will awoke early in the morning, with the moon still high in a dark, murky sky. He snatched up the book of Thomas Gray's poetry he'd begun reading again and silently crept down to the hall. He settled into the deep wing-backed chair near the fireplace, which held only cold, gray ashes. In spite of Nellie's reminder to Toby, the fire hadn't been banked.

No matter, Will thought. The air was cool but not chilly.

Lost in the beauty of the words he was reading, Will was startled when Toby suddenly appeared at his side, concerned because the fire was out.

Will watched Toby take the flint and striker from the cabinet and scrape them together until sparks flew, lighting a new fire.

"Toby," Will said, "you must be careful. My brother John told our father that he thought he heard you talking to the prisoners. I told them you had been talking to me."

Toby dropped the flint and striker, and fear filled his eyes. As he scrambled to pick up the tools, he said, "I best get back to helpin' Nellie in the kitchen."

Will was surprised by Toby's behavior. Didn't Toby realize that Will was trying to help him? Why wouldn't Toby trust him?

Behind Will a floorboard made a popping sound, and he stiffened, thinking at first it was a footstep. Had Papa overheard? Will twisted, leaning out of his chair, then sighed with relief when he saw that no one was there.

The members of his family would awaken soon, so Will worked hard at his chores. With Nellie's cooking scenting the air, Will eagerly lugged the heavy buckets of water and the metal cup through the passage for the thirsty prisoners.

Alice Field stared through the bars with swollen, reddened eyes. "How long must we wait for the General Court?" she begged. "How many days?" Her hands shook as she accepted the cup of water.

"Twelve days," Will told her, "but civil cases will be heard first, my father said. Criminal cases are always heard last."

Margaret Turnbull spoke up behind her. "The

71

children of the old gentleman I cared for in his last illness claimed I stole eight silver forks, a pitcher, and a serving plate from his home. I did not. It was when his sister visited that the pieces went missing."

Miss Field snickered. "If that is your story, I hope you have hidden them well."

Tears flooded Mrs. Turnbull's eyes. "I told you, I did not take the old man's property. There are those who will testify to my innocence."

As Miss Field laughed again, Mrs. Turnbull gripped the bars. "Young Will," she said, "what does your father say about my chances for acquittal?"

"I don't know. We haven't talked about it," Will answered as he handed her a cup of water.

"Will you ask him for me? I must know."

Will nodded. "Yes, Mrs. Turnbull. I'll ask him."

Mrs. Turnbull's eyes were so sorrowful, her spirits so downcast, that Will wanted with all his heart to believe her. He hoped the judge and jury would acquit her.

Will did not stop to talk at the men's cell. He had no time to waste. He badly needed to speak to Joseph. Joseph would know what he should do.

The family's gathering at the breakfast table was subdued. Mr. Pelham seemed distracted. He drummed his fingers on the table and ate very little. Remembering their father's warning that he would continue to read the rules from the *School of Manners* if there was any misbehavior, the Pelham children ate quietly and carefully. Henry did not spill his cup of milk.

Will worked hard at his penmanship and the studies his mother gave him, then took the prisoners their midday meal—wooden bowls of hominy cooked with a ham bone. Tiny flecks of gristle and fat, boiled from the bone, speckled the hominy.

After he'd collected the empty bowls and carried them to Nellie to be washed, Will slipped from the yard and ran down Nicholson Street to Joseph's house.

"I was just coming to find you," Joseph told Will. "Let's go to the brickmaker's yard on Henry Street. His apprentices are treading down the clay now in their bare feet." Joseph clutched Will's arm with excitement. " 'Tis a wonder how they do it. Stomp, stomp, stomp, to drive the bubbles out of the clay, and all the while the wet, sticky mud squishes up between the toes."

Will perked up. "Do you think they will let us help stomp?"

Joseph shrugged. "If they won't let us help, at least we may watch."

Will shook his head, suddenly remembering why he had come. "First I need to talk with you," he said.

Joseph led the way to a grassy patch behind his house. He plopped down and waited until Will sat beside him.

"What's wrong?" Joseph asked.

Will took a long, deep, shuddering breath. Then he told Joseph all he knew about Mills Mansfield, who could be sentenced to be hanged; and Emmanuel, who dreaded being returned to his master or sold.

"Joseph," Will said solemnly, "after the family was asleep last night I went down the stairs to find Toby to warn him that my brother John had overheard him talking to the prisoners."

Joseph's eyes opened wide. "Did he admit it?"

"Yes. No. That is, I knew he'd been talking to Emmanuel. I heard him. But last night I didn't tell Toby anything. I stopped on the stairs because he was speaking to Nellie. He said something about 'where to go when a man escapes.' "

Joseph sat up straight. "You heard Toby talking to Emmanuel yourself? And now he's speaking of escape? Where did he say to go?"

"He didn't. I heard only part of a sentence. Nellie told Toby not to say things like that, and Toby told her something about how men had a right to be free. I think he was talking about Emmanuel. I left then and ran upstairs to my bedchamber. I don't know what else Toby said."

Joseph thought a moment. "Have you heard Toby say anything about Emmanuel escaping?"

"No."

"Are you sure you heard him talking to Emmanuel?"

"I've seen him near the prisoners, but I don't know what was said. Slaves are forbidden to talk to the prisoners. Papa said this has always been one of the rules."

Joseph studied Will. "Are you going to tell your father?"

Will groaned and said, "I can't."

"You have no real reason to think Emmanuel is planning to escape."

The pressure in Will's chest began to slide away. "Do you really believe so?" he asked.

"Think about it, Will," Joseph argued. "The only times the prisoners are out of their cells are when they're taken to the exercise yard. And Emmanuel would still be in leg irons. There is no way he could escape while wearing those heavy irons."

Will wanted to believe what Joseph was telling him. It made perfect sense. But he still had doubts.

Joseph cocked his head, once again studying Will. "You don't believe me? Or is there something about Toby and Emmanuel you haven't told me?"

Will shrugged. "I didn't hear anything said about an actual escape. Toby was talking about 'when a man escapes,' as if it were something to just think about. But there was a kind of feeling in the air. Do you know what I mean?"

"A feeling in the air?" Joseph grinned. "You're as bad as old Jake. Isn't his pirate ghost planning an escape? Maybe that's who you should be worried about."

Joseph jumped to his feet and held out a hand to Will. "Come on," he said. "Race you to the brickmaker's yard."

Will put Toby and Emmanuel out of his mind and ran after Joseph to Henry Street, stopping only when they reached the brickyard, where a wooden form held the wet clay.

Just as Joseph had said, the cold, mushy clay squished up in wonderful, lumpy swirls through the apprentices' toes. Will was disappointed when the brickyard owner turned down Joseph's offer to help.

Will leaned against a post, watching the treaders. "I wish . . . ," he said, then stopped speaking.

Joseph turned to him. "You wish what?"

"I wish I knew more about how slavery got started in the Virginia colony."

Staring at Will in surprise, Joseph asked, "Why would you want to know something like that?"

"I don't know. Sometimes I find slavery hard to understand."

"What's hard to understand?"

"Why some people should be slaves and some should be free."

Joseph looked surprised. "That's just the way it is."

"But is that the way it's supposed to be?" Will asked.

He frowned as he thought. "My mother said she's heard that Thomas Jefferson has questioned slavery."

A mischievous gleam sparked in Joseph's eyes, and the corners of his mouth twitched. "Then why don't you ask your questions of Thomas Jefferson?"

"Ask him? Are you daft? Thomas Jefferson is a burgess. He wouldn't talk to a gaoler's son."

"I think he would," Joseph said, "and I know how you can find out if you're right or I am. Let's visit Mr. Southall at the tavern."

Will hesitated. "Are you sure this is a good idea?"

Grabbing Will's arm, Joseph gave him a tug. "Come with me to the Raleigh. We'll see if Mr. Jefferson is there."

Shy now about talking to Mr. Jefferson and half hoping he wouldn't be there, Will ran with Joseph to the side door of Raleigh Tavern. He'd visited the tavern when Joseph's father owned it, proud because many important people in Virginia dined there with friends.

Mr. James Southall, a filled tray in his hands, looked surprised as Joseph entered the passage. "What can I do for you lads?" he asked pleasantly.

"Is Mr. Thomas Jefferson here, sir?" Joseph asked.

"As a matter of fact, he is," Mr. Southall said. "Has someone sent you here with a message to give to him?"

"No, sir," Joseph said. "Will and I . . . we just want to take a look at him."

"Very well. You may watch him from the passage here, but see that it comes to no more than that," Mr. Southall answered. "Mr. Jefferson is in an important discussion with friends, and he's not to be interrupted. Is that understood?"

"Yes, sir," Will and Joseph said together.

Will found himself breathing a long sigh of relief, yet at the same time he felt a touch of disappointment. Much as he feared actually talking to Mr. Jefferson and was glad he'd been ordered not to, at the same time he wanted very much to know what Mr. Jefferson thought about slavery and how slaves would care for themselves if they were freed.

Will knew there were slave owners who, on occasion, sought permission from the governor and the council to free a slave. But he had often heard grown-ups say that black people did not think as white people did, that they needed to be cared for. If this were true, then how could Emmanuel take care of himself . . . *if* he escaped?

Joseph tugged Will over to a doorway and pushed him into a crouching position. "There he is! The man with the red hair and the long legs sticking out at the side of his table!"

Will stared at Thomas Jefferson and the three

other men who sat at a table near the fireplace, so close to where he and Joseph were hiding that it was possible to hear some of the conversation.

The men were discussing one of the civil cases that would be heard during the upcoming General Court. Will soon began to feel uncomfortable listening to this private conversation. He pulled at Joseph's sleeve. "I'm leaving," he whispered.

He rose and hurried down the passageway and out the back door.

Joseph caught up with Will, jumping off the back step and running to his side. "Why did you leave? Did you not want to hear what Thomas Jefferson and his friends were saying?"

"No, I didn't," Will said. He kicked at a pile of red and gold leaves that had drifted to the ground. "I felt as if I were spying."

"We *were* spying," Joseph admitted. "I've spied in that passage since I was a small boy."

Will turned to look at his friend. "But we're no longer small boys." Trying to answer Joseph's puzzled gaze, Will added, "We are old enough to think about what we are doing and understand why we are doing it. The decisions we make now affect more than just ourselves. Do you know what I mean?"

"I know what you are saying," Joseph answered, "and I know this is what we must do someday . . .

but not now. With five brothers and sisters, I wish to remain a child for as long as possible. I don't wish to take on the heavy responsibilities of being a man."

Will wished he had the same choice. But with his responsibilities at the gaol, he knew his own childhood was already behind him.

With a laugh, Joseph gave Will a shove. "We are being much too serious," he said. "I'll race you back to my house!"

Will ran, too, struggling to get ahead of Joseph. He arrived at the house right behind his friend. Both boys flung themselves on the grass, panting and laughing.

Joseph rolled onto his back, gazing up at the sky. "It grows dark early," he said.

"You're right!" Will sat up, startled. "I'll be late for my evening chores."

"Your parents won't mind too much, will they?" Joseph asked.

"Not too much," Will called back, but he ran as fast as he could for his home. His mother would worry about where he had gone. Worst of all, not only he, but the entire family, would probably have to listen to another long list of rules of proper behavior.

Chapter Eight

Will was right. Before supper Mr. Pelham opened his copy of the *School of Manners*.

Sarah sighed loudly. "Papa," she said, "do we all have to hear the rules just because Will was late for his evening chores?"

"These are rules for all children to learn and re-member," Mr. Pelham said, as Mrs. Pelham nodded agreement. " 'Twill not harm you to hear them."

John scowled and kicked Will's leg under the table. "I'm hungry, Papa, and I am not at fault because Will was late. Why should I have to hear the rules?"

Mr. Pelham leaned toward John and answered firmly, "Boys who kick their brothers in anger should pay special attention to rule number six."

Will reminded himself that it was his own fault

Papa was reading the rules of behavior. His father seemed unhappy, and Will knew his tardiness must be the reason.

He didn't blame his brothers and sisters, either, for the way they felt. He'd make it up to the two little ones by playing a game of horsie with them after supper, hoisting them one at a time to his back and galloping around the room.

Elizabeth loved the game and always shrieked loudly. Mama and Papa never seemed to mind the noise.

Finally, Mr. Pelham cleared his throat. " 'The Short and Mixt Precepts,' " he read.

"Short? I hope they're really short," John whispered.

" 'Number one, fear God,' " Mr. Pelham read. " 'Number two, Honor the King. Number three, Reverence thy Parents. Number four, Submit to thy Superiors. Number five, Despise not thy Inferiors. Number six, Be courteous with thy Equals.' "

Equals . . . slaves . . . escape.

Mr. Pelham kept reading, but Will stopped paying close attention. He had a lot on his mind.

Finally Mr. Pelham closed the book with a snap and laid it beside his fork. "Nellie, you may bring in the food," he said. But in turn he looked into the eyes of each of his children. "I hope you have profited by learning these rules," he said.

"Yes, Papa. Thank you, Papa," Sarah said sweetly.

"Yes, thank you, Papa," Elizabeth echoed.

Girls can be sickening, Will thought, then jumped when his father spoke suddenly to him. "Which rule do you think can best benefit you, Will?"

Frantically Will searched his mind, grabbing the first thought that came past. " 'Hearken to instruction,' " he said, wondering where the thought came from and whether it was one of the rules Papa had read.

Mr. Pelham smiled. "Rule number ten. A good choice," he said.

"Papa," John asked, "why did you tell us those were short and mixed precepts? They were mixed, all right, but they were not short."

Mrs. Pelham laughed and reached to hug John. "Dear ones," she said, "you will soon be the best-behaved children in Williamsburg."

John scowled. "If we are, it will be Will's fault."

Nellie accepted the plates of pork sausage and baked eggs from Mr. Pelham, placing them in front of the family members.

Will scarcely waited until his father had said the blessing before he hungrily began to eat.

After supper, in the flickering candlelight, Mrs. Pelham asked Will to take John to bed earlier than usual. "I am very tired," she said. " 'Tis time we all had a good night's rest."

Mr. Pelham arranged a branched candlestick on the desk in the corner. "I will come to bed later," he said. "I must go over a few accounts."

As Will held his candlestick high, lighting the way down the passage to the stairs, Mrs. Turnbull called to him, "Will? Did you ask your father?"

It took Will a moment to remember what she had said earlier. His cheeks grew hot with embarrassment. The poor woman was so frightened and worried, and he had forgotten her request to ask his father if he thought she had a chance at acquittal.

Remembering that his father would be in the hall working, Will quickly answered, "I will ask him within a few minutes, Mrs. Turnbull. First I must put my brother to bed."

"I can put myself to bed," John insisted. He ran a few steps ahead, still careful to remain within the circle of light.

John was drowsy and Will knew he'd soon fall asleep, so Will took the candle with him and returned to the hall.

"Papa?" he said softly as he approached his father's desk.

Mr. Pelham glanced up, and Will could see the exhaustion in his eyes. It was not fair to interrupt his father's work, but Will had promised Mrs. Turnbull.

"Papa," Will continued, "Mrs. Turnbull wants to know if you think there is a chance she'll be found innocent and set free."

Mr. Pelham rubbed his eyes and the sides of his face before he answered. "The judge and jury will hear the evidence and make their decision," he said. "That is all I know."

"You told me you thought Jake would be set free."

"That is true. I did." Mr. Pelham sighed. "I understand there are also witnesses for Margaret Turnbull—people for whom she has worked. She has never stolen before, and they insist she did not steal the items for which she is charged."

"Mrs. Turnbull said the things went missing after the old man's sister came to visit."

Mr. Pelham sighed. "It will be the sister's word against Mrs. Turnbull's . . . and Mrs. Turnbull's friends."

Will felt discouraged. "Is there nothing to give her a word of hope?"

"I do not want to give her false hope."

"Is that the only hope there is?"

For a moment Mr. Pelham bent his head and rubbed his eyes again. Then he said, "Tell Mrs. Turnbull her friends will come to testify for her good character. In General Court, she will be given a fair trial and the truth will be told."

Will thought a moment. Surely there was hope to be had from this—a fair trial and the chance to come out with the truth. "Thank you, Papa," he said.

The door of his parents' bedchamber opened, and his mother came into the room. "I heard talking," she said. "Why are you not in bed, Will?"

"I had to ask Papa a question about one of the prisoners," Will answered.

"Is the prisoner ill? In need of medication?"

"No. She had a question about the General Court."

"Well then, run along, child," Mrs. Pelham told him. "You can talk to your father about it in the morning." She leaned to give him a kiss on the cheek.

"Good night, Mama," Will said. "Good night, Papa."

He walked quietly into the passage, but he stopped as he heard his father say, "Will asked the fate of one of the women prisoners—Margaret Turnbull. The woman was charged with grand larceny, and the penalty for that could be hanging."

Will stiffened, leaning against the wall. Carefully he shielded the flame of his candle.

His father's voice dropped, but Will could still hear him clearly. "Ann, I do not wish to see anyone condemned to death, but I dread what will happen if someone pleads benefit of clergy. I become physically ill thinking about the possibility of being called up before the judges to burn the hand of one of the prisoners."

"Oh, my dear husband, I know how inflicting pain must hurt you. But carrying out the punishment for a crime is only one of your jobs as gaoler," Mrs. Pelham said. "I am proud of you for taking this occupation in order to care for your family."

Will knew his mother was trying to comfort his father, but her voice shook and there was no strength in her words.

"I am a man who loves music and beauty. I cannot inflict pain on another human being," Mr. Pelham said.

"Surely, to escape hanging, those prisoners who are able will ask for benefit of clergy," Mrs. Pelham said. "You must keep in mind that even though they will suffer temporary pain by being branded, their lives will be spared."

In the silence that followed, Will remembered what Mills Mansfield had said about asking for benefit of clergy if he should be convicted of forgery. Will winced.

Mr. Pelham finally spoke. His voice was calmer. "Madam, you have given me good advice," he said. "I will keep your words in mind."

"Come to bed, sir," Mrs. Pelham said. "You need your rest."

"You are a good wife," Mr. Pelham answered.

Will walked quickly down the passage until he arrived at the women's cell. "Mrs. Turnbull?" he whispered.

"Yes?" Her face was pressed against the bars. "What did your father say?"

Will took a deep breath before he spoke, trying to sound hopeful. "He said you have friends who are coming to testify in your behalf. You worked for them, and they wish to tell the judge and jury about your honesty. My father said our English laws are just. You will have a fair trial, and everyone will hear the truth."

"Thank you," Mrs. Turnbull whispered. "You are a good boy, and I will dwell on what you have told me. I trust in my friends and in the truth and in God."

Will plodded down the passage and up the stairs to his bedchamber. He wasn't sleepy. Even after he had removed all his clothes except for his shirt, he lay in bed staring wide-eyed at the ceiling.

He ached for his father and for Mrs. Turnbull and for Mills Mansfield.

"Blackbeard," Will whispered aloud, "if you really are here and you really are planning to escape, please take Margaret Turnbull and Mills Mansfield with you."

Chapter Nine

As the date of General Court approached, Will could see his father trying with great difficulty to hide his worries. The other Pelham children didn't understand why their father was at times moody and at other times a little cross, but Will knew. Peter Pelham dreaded the role he would have to play in the punishment assigned to the prisoners.

To make matters much worse, there was the possibility that some of the prisoners would try to escape. If they succeeded, Will's father could be held accountable. Will felt as if two carriages were racing at top speed toward each other and he was powerless to stop them. What could he do?

On Saturday, before Will took the prisoners their meal at midday, Mr. Pelham said, "There will be one less prisoner to feed on Thursday of next week, Will. A Mr. Roger Alberson, from New Brunswick County, was notified of the advertisement about Emmanuel and had a letter sent to me, claiming to be his owner."

Will gasped. "Papa! Emmanuel will be sent back?"

"No. Mr. Alberson will travel here to Williamsburg during Public Times. He'll arrive on October seventeenth to claim and take charge of his slave."

Will shook his head, trying to clear it of the horrible thoughts that came to mind. "Papa, Mr. Alberson beat Emmanuel until he nearly died! Once he takes him away, he will surely kill him, he will be so angry that Emmanuel ran from him."

Mr. Pelham rested a hand on Will's shoulder. "Just as you do, I deplore any man's being cruel to a slave, but we do not know if Emmanuel's story is true. Even if it is, we have no legal right to interfere with Mr. Alberson's treatment of Emmanuel. He has purchased the slave, who is now his property to do with as he wishes."

Will sucked in his breath. "Is that not wrong?" he asked.

Mr. Pelham studied Will. "Are you asking if mistreatment is wrong or if slavery is wrong?"

Hesitating, Will finally answered, "I don't know, Papa. You take good care of Nellie and Toby, and Mama needs their help. But Emmanuel . . . I don't think he should go back to an owner who will surely kill him."

"Now, Will," Mr. Pelham said, "there is nothing but Emmanuel's word to prove that Mr. Alberson beat him as badly as Emmanuel claims. Mr. Alberson wrote a courteous, well-mannered letter to me, without anger or disdain for his slave. I think Emmanuel must feel guilty for running away from his master and therefore has simply given in to childlike fears."

"Emmanuel is not a child. He's a grown man."

"He's a slave. It is well known that slaves, women, and children need others to guide them."

Will knew there was no point in arguing with his father when he wasn't sure himself what he believed. "Does Emmanuel know his owner will be coming for him?" he asked.

"Yes," Mr. Pelham answered. "I told him as soon as I received the letter this morning." He hesitated, then added, "He did not take the news well."

Later, when Will brought food to the prisoners, Emmanuel did not come to the slot to receive his share. Will looked through the bars and saw Emmanuel slumped on a pile of hay, his head resting on his hands.

"Emmanuel," he called, "here is your meal."

Emmanuel's back heaved in a shuddering sigh, but he didn't answer.

"Are you not hungry?" Will asked.

Mansfield stepped up to the bars and accepted the bowl. "I'll take this to him," he told Will.

Will watched as Mansfield sat next to Emmanuel and told him, "Eat to keep up your strength. No one has ever survived a journey on an empty stomach."

Earnestly Will added, "That's right. And 'tis a long road to New Brunswick County."

Emmanuel raised his head. For one long moment he looked at Will. Then he turned to Mansfield, who held out the bowl of hominy. Emmanuel silently took it and began to eat.

Will turned away from the bars. Emmanuel's eyes were puffed and swollen and his gaze deep and watery, like the gaze of someone looking up from the bottom of a pool. Will had never seen anyone so stricken with grief, and it frightened him. What if Emmanuel was right? What if his owner would claim him only to kill him?

Will turned to leave, but Jake pressed his face against the bars, whispering, "Will, come closer."

As Will hesitated, Jake grew more insistent. "Come—and be quiet about it. I have something important to tell you."

Curiosity overcame Will's aversion to Jake's stinking breath. He stepped close to the cell's door, turning his head so that Jake could whisper in his ear.

"Do not carry such worry in your heart about Emmanuel. His owner will not harm him."

Startled, Will turned to Jake. "How do you know this?"

"Shhh!" Jake replied, and Will winced at the rancid odor that hit him directly in the face.

Jake smiled and waggled a finger. "Blackbeard will see that Emmanuel comes to no harm. He will lead him far away from here."

Will slumped. He should have known that nothing old Jake had to say would help.

"So be of good cheer," Jake said. His cackle followed Will down the passage.

Will had little time to puzzle over Jake's strange message because he was kept busy the rest of the day running errands. Just when he thought he was finished, his mother sent him to John Greenhow's store to purchase an iron trivet and to William Rind's *Virginia Gazette* office to pick up the printed sheets of music his father had ordered for his students. She did not say "Hurry back," so as Will passed Joseph's house he knocked at the door.

When Joseph opened the door, Will explained his errands and said, "Come with me."

"Right away," Joseph answered. He reached for his coat, then stopped. "We'll probably meet Robert at the store," he said. "Aunt Peachy is in the parlor having tea with Mama, who will insist we keep Robert with us."

" 'Tis no matter," Will said. He hoped he would have at least a few minutes in which he could freely talk to Joseph before Robert came along. He needed to tell Joseph his fears for Emmanuel.

Joseph went to inform his mother he was leaving, and Will stepped outside to wait. The fall air was crisp and cool, and rustling leaves were turning to brilliant golds and reds and oranges. Will took two long, deep breaths, soaking up the dry, spicy fragrance of fall. Soon there would be pumpkins, mashed and cooked into fritters with sugar and spices; late apples to be sliced and sugared and baked into tarts; and maybe even venison pasty.

But Wednesday, October 16, the opening of the General Court, would arrive in just a few days. Will shivered.

Joseph, who had stepped from the porch behind him, glanced at Will with curiosity. "Are you cold?" he asked.

"No," Will answered. He began to walk with Joseph toward Mr. Rind's printing office on Duke of Gloucester Street. "I was thinking about what Jake told me."

Joseph's eyes sparkled, and he began to grin. "What fine story about Jake do you have today?" he asked.

"Jake has been talking about Blackbeard again," he said.

Joseph snickered. "What did the old pirate ghost do this time?"

"This time it's about Emmanuel," Will said. "Emmanuel's owner has written to my father. He told him he'd come to claim Emmanuel on Thursday of next week. The second day that the General Court will be in session."

Will took a long breath. "The news about his owner has made Emmanuel grieve. He is sure this time his owner will kill him. I felt very sad seeing Emmanuel suffer, but Jake told me not to worry. He said Blackbeard would see that Emmanuel would come to no harm, that he would lead him far away from the gaol."

Joseph stopped and stared at Will. "What does that mean?"

"I don't know. At first I thought it was just one of Jake's fanciful wishes. But then I wondered if it could be true. If Emmanuel is planning to escape, I need to tell my father."

"Don't be daft, Will. Jake is full of unlikely stories, like the one about telling Colonel Washington how to fight a battle."

Will thought about the way Jake's eyes had brightened and how he'd told the story with pride. "It seemed true as he told it," he answered.

Joseph scoffed. "If you'd believe that, then you'd have to believe his Blackbeard stories are true."

Joseph wiggled his fingers at Will as he bent over and crept around him. "Booooo," he moaned. "I'm Blackbeard, the ghost of the public gaol, and I will get you!"

"Are you still telling Blackbeard stories?" Robert asked as he joined them.

"We have no way of proving whether Jake's stories are true or not," Will said seriously.

"Yes, you have. You can find out," Robert said.

Will and Joseph stared at him.

"How can we find out?" Will asked.

"My father said that Colonel Washington is visiting in Williamsburg again today. He and his friends have gone to Raleigh Tavern for a pipe and dinner before attending a play at the theater."

As Will and Joseph continued to stare, Robert said, "If you really want to know if the story Jake told about Washington is true, you could go to the tavern and ask the colonel himself."

Actually speak to the great Colonel Washington? Will gulped. "Very well," he said. "I will do that."

Joseph stepped up beside him and placed a hand on Will's shoulder. "Then I will go with you."

"You don't need to."

"I want to go with you," Joseph said. "I want to see your face when Colonel Washington laughs at you."

"You're very sure you are right."

"I am."

Will shrugged. "Right or wrong, I need to know if the story is true. Let's go."

"Me too," Robert insisted.

Will put an arm around Robert's plump shoulders. "You too, Robert," he said.

A few minutes later, as they neared Raleigh Tavern, Will said, "I hope Mr. Southall doesn't forbid us to speak to Colonel Washington."

Robert answered before Joseph had a chance to. "I have a plan. I will engage Mr. Southall in conversation, while you and Joseph sneak into the tavern."

"Sneak?" Will repeated. Was this how he wanted to meet the great Colonel Washington?

"I'll show you how to do it," Joseph said.

Will shook his head. "No. We will walk into Raleigh Tavern and right up to Colonel Washington's table. If Mr. Southall asks us to leave, we will, but first we may get an answer from Colonel Washington."

While Robert seemed skeptical, Joseph looked at Will with admiration. "Very well," he said. "I'll be right beside you."

Will was content. Colonel Washington's answer could put his mind at ease. If Jake had made up this story, then his stories about Blackbeard and Emmanuel must be just as fanciful, and there would be nothing to worry about. He hoped with all his heart that Joseph was right and Colonel Washington would laugh at the story.

In spite of his brave words, as they arrived at the tavern, Will ducked through the back door after Joseph and Robert and followed them into the passage.

As they arrived at the doorway to the main room, Joseph stopped so suddenly that Robert walked into him.

"Watch what you're doing," Robert scolded.

"Shhh!" Joseph held a finger to his lips. He whispered to Will, "There is Colonel George Washington, sitting in the same chair that Thomas Jefferson sat in, close to the fireplace." He grinned and added, "And Mr. Southall is nowhere in sight."

Will stood as tall as he could and said, "Then let's do what we came to do." Stepping past Joseph and Robert, Will led the way to George Washington's side.

Colonel Washington and the two men with him looked up in surprise.

Remembering the good manners his parents had taught him, Will bowed and said, "Good day to you, Colonel Washington, sir. I am your obedient servant, William Pelham, son of Peter Pelham, the organist at Bruton Parish Church and gaoler at the public gaol."

"I am pleased to make your acquaintance, William," Colonel Washington said, rising and bow-ing. He glanced at Joseph and Robert. "And these young men?"

"My friends Joseph Hay and Robert Greenhow." Will paused, not knowing how to follow the rules of behavior and still tell his story.

"Colonel Washington," he said, "my father makes our family listen to . . . that is, he reads to us the rules of behavior from a book of good manners. Rule number one is 'Among superiors speak not till thou art asked.' But how can you ask me to speak if you don't know what I want to speak to you about?"

"That is a question well put," Colonel Washington said. "We shall settle the matter now. Pray tell me what you have in mind."

Before he could answer, Will's shoulders were caught in a painful grip, and a voice over his head said, "I beg your pardon, gentlemen. These young rapscallions should not have annoyed you. I will send them packing immediately."

Colonel Washington held up a hand. "There seems to be some confusion, Mr. Southall. I have invited them to speak with me. I pray you to allow their presence in your tavern, sir."

Will was released so suddenly that he struggled to maintain his balance.

"Of course, Colonel Washington!" Mr. Southall

exclaimed. "I hope you will accept my apologies, sir, for interrupting."

"Thank you, Colonel Washington," Will said as soon as Mr. Southall had left. He took a deep breath and quickly said, "This is what I must ask you. A farmer named Jake Sample is in the public gaol. Do you remember him, sir?"

Colonel Washington looked puzzled and shook his head, so Will went on to tell him Jake's story about giving the colonel a drink of water and suggesting that Colonel Washington's troops round up the French the way Jake and his dog rounded up sheep.

One of the men at the table grinned. The other guffawed. Joseph, too, had a smug look on his face. Will was about to turn away, but Colonel Washington smiled and said, "I do remember the incident, although I had long ago forgotten Mr. Sample's name."

"You jest, sir," one of his friends said.

"Not at all," Colonel Washington answered. "It happened in the spring of the year 1755. I was unable to use Mr. Sample's tactics in our battles with the French, but I could see that under certain circumstances the technique might prove to be of value."

Joseph's mouth fell open. "The story is true? It really happened?"

Colonel Washington smiled at Will, Joseph, and Robert in turn. "It did," he said. "Mr. Sample told the truth. Do you have any more questions for me?"

"No, sir," Will answered, shaken by Colonel Washington's answer. "Thank you, Colonel Washington."

One man at the table took his long-stemmed pipe from his mouth and chuckled. "Mr. Southall is looking this way, lads. If I were you, I'd scamper."

Will, Joseph, and Robert bowed and backed away as quickly as they could. As soon as they had left the main room of the tavern, Robert took off at a run, Joseph hurrying after him. But Will walked out of the tavern as he had walked in, his mind on the many things Jake Sample had said.

Colonel Washington had not told Will what he'd wished to hear. It seemed that Jake was not just a fanciful teller of tales. Even though Jake's stories were colored with hints and secrets and strange characters like Blackbeard, apparently he spoke the truth. At least, he had this time.

Blackbeard was leaving the gaol and would take Emmanuel with him, Jake had said. Was an escape really planned for Emmanuel? Could Blackbeard protect him from his cruel owner?

Will's head ached with the puzzle. How could an old pirate ghost arrange for a successful escape?

Chapter Ten

Will returned home silently, placing the purchases from the store and the printer on a table in the hall. As quietly as possible, he stole into the passage. He discovered to his dismay that Toby was again at the cell door, speaking with a prisoner.

As a floorboard creaked under Will's foot, Toby started. His eyes widened when he saw Will. Without a word, Toby quickly left the cells. As he passed, Toby looked down, not meeting Will's eyes.

Suddenly Will had a thought: *Could Toby be Blackbeard?*

Will hoped with all his heart that he wasn't. If Toby helped another slave escape, he would immediately be arrested, and the penalty was death.

Could one of the other prisoners be Blackbeard? Maybe Mills Mansfield?

Will shook his head. He hoped not. Death was the penalty for forgery, but Mansfield had said that because he had never before been convicted of a crime, he could escape the sentence by pleading benefit of clergy. The branding on the heel of his thumb would be painful, but at least he would be free.

Perhaps one of the other prisoners was Blackbeard. Colin Campbell, who'd been arrested for the crime of maiming, was certainly mean enough to take on the identity of the old pirate.

Or how about John King, who had committed a felony? Or Thomas Welch? Horse stealing was a felony, too. Both of these crimes carried the penalty of death. Either of these men could be desperate enough to plan an escape.

Lying on the counterpane in his bedchamber, Will stopped trying to think about who might plan the escape and told himself that, just as Joseph had said, escape was well nigh impossible. Emmanuel wore leg irons, connected with a short length of chain that made it hard to walk, let alone run. The leg irons were riveted and couldn't be removed until Will's father used his hammer and chisel to cut through them.

The doors of the cells were sturdy and heavy, with stout locks. Even though the prisoners were allowed to exercise in the small yard outside their cells each afternoon, they were kept from leaving by the high brick wall that enclosed the yard on three sides.

The puzzle was too much for Will to solve. *I'll have to tell Papa all that I've learned,* he thought. *Even though I have nothing to offer but my suspicions, he does need to know.*

But that evening, during supper, Mr. Pelham seemed even more distracted and nervous than he had been. "This is already Saturday, the twelfth, and the opening day of court is on Wednesday—in less than four days," he announced, as if he were reconfirming the dates to himself.

Mrs. Pelham calmly picked up her spoon to dip into her bowl of pea soup. "Will brought home the music you ordered from William Rind," she said.

"The music? Oh, the music. Thank you, Will," Mr. Pelham said.

"And he brought the trivet I needed from John Greenhow's store."

Mr. Pelham managed a smile. "You were a busy lad this afternoon, son," he said, dropping his soup spoon with a clatter. It was obvious he was nervous about the first opening of General Court that he would officially attend. It wouldn't help to give him even more to worry about—worries that would probably turn out to be worth nothing at all.

So Will merely nodded. He wished he could tell his

father about his visit with Colonel George Washington. He had intended to do so and to tell him that this proved Jake's tales were based on truth. But then Will would have to tell the rest, including his suspicions that there might be an attempted escape from the gaol.

He couldn't. They were only suspicions. He had no proof at all. If he told his father that Toby had been speaking with Emmanuel, Toby would be in terrible trouble. And, for all he knew, Toby was only trying to be a friend to the runaway slave.

Will bent over his soup, slurping loudly before he remembered the rule he was supposed to keep in mind about never making loud noises at the table. He quickly looked at his parents to see if they had noticed. But his mother was busy helping little Henry to hold his spoon properly, and his father had not glanced up from his plate.

With the exception of Elizabeth's and Henry's chatter, the meal was a quiet one. Will eagerly looked forward to the days after the General Court had ended. By that time the other prisoners would have been tried and sentenced, and the Pelham family's daily life would return to normal. In the near future there would be other prisoners to fill the gaol, until the criminal trials at the Courts of Oyer and Terminer in December. But surely none of them would be so worrisome as those now in the gaol.

With Mrs. Pelham's reminder that the morrow was Sunday, which meant an early rising, the family prepared for bed soon after supper.

Once again, Will took John down the passage to their room. The men's cell was silent, but as they passed the women's cell, Miss Field called out in a quavery voice, "How many days until the trials, Will?"

"The civil trials will be heard first, then the criminal. Your trial could be held on any date on or after October sixteenth."

Her voice was insistent. "How many days until then?"

"Four."

"Four long days," Miss Field wailed. She began to sniffle.

Will hurried his brother up to the bedchamber and settled him into bed. When John was comfortable, Will took off all his clothes but his shirt and climbed into his own bed, ready for sleep.

But sleep wouldn't come. There were questions that must be answered. Perhaps if he spoke again with Jake, he could learn more than he had thus far from the prisoner's bewildering riddles. Will was fairly certain that Jake did not think of Blackbeard as anything more than a ghost. However, maybe he would heedlessly say something that might give a clue as to the identity of the person pretending to be Blackbeard.

Impatiently Will waited for Sarah to fall asleep. At long last her breathing slowed and became steady and he climbed out of bed. The bedchamber was dark, with barely a touch of moonlight, but Will easily found his breeches where he had left them. He slipped them on and buttoned them.

Shoes would make noise, and stockings were not important—the floorboards were not chill enough to matter. Will did not light a candle. He didn't want to be discovered in the passage. Satisfying himself that his brother and sister were sleeping soundly and would not be disturbed, he silently opened the door and walked carefully down the edges of the stair treads, where the boards would not creak under his weight.

He slipped along the passage, scarcely breathing, hoping that Miss Field would not hear him. He tried to be polite, but her constant questioning and crying made him cringe. As Will passed the women's cell and all was silent, he let out a sigh of relief.

Approaching the barred window in the door of the men's cell, Will hesitated. Was that whispering he heard? Were people talking?

Will crept as close as he could, knowing that in the dark he could not be seen.

"Where will you go?"

Will recognized Jake's raspy voice. At first he stiffened, wondering if Jake had discovered his presence.

But as the voice continued, Will knew Jake was speaking to someone else.

"You will not be safe. Men and dogs will come looking for you."

A low, deep voice answered. "I am the great Blackbeard. I fear no man. And I warn you, Jake Sample, do not tell the plans you have heard to anyone—especially to Will."

Will gasped in shock. Staggering backward into the opposite wall of the passage, he leaned against it for support. His knees wobbled. His throat grew dry. With his own ears, he had heard Blackbeard speak.

Blackbeard wasn't a ghost. He *was* an actual person.

A bolt of recognition, as powerful as a thunderclap, shook Will. He knew the voice of the man who posed as Blackbeard. He remembered, when he had first heard Jake speak of Blackbeard, Mills Mansfield's imitation of the pirate's swagger, and the very words "I am the great Blackbeard."

It was Mansfield who intended to escape with Emmanuel!

But how? Even if they were able to leave the goal, they couldn't go far with Emmanuel in leg irons.

Would they go together? Separately? Will thought hard. Two separate escapes wouldn't work. Maybe the first to leave would get away, but his father and the sheriff would become more alert, and the second prisoner who tried to escape wouldn't have a chance. Mansfield and Emmanuel would have to travel together.

But at some point, Will knew, they would separate. Two trails would be more difficult to follow than one.

Will slumped, sliding down to sit cross-legged on the floor, as he realized how much he wanted the escape to succeed.

Emmanuel was Roger Alberson's property. There was no legal doubt about it. But Emmanuel shouldn't have to suffer the cruelties of his owner.

As for Mills Mansfield, he had done the wrong thing by forging his employer's signature for a payment that was rightfully owed him. But Will liked Mansfield and hated to think of him suffering either the sentence of death or a painful branding as the result. 'Twould be better to escape whatever punishment the court would give him.

Suffering from his mixed-up feelings, Will faced the truth. He knew how faithfully his father trusted him. His job was to assist his father, and he carried the heavy responsibility of this task. He realized that he must do what was right, and helping prisoners to escape by keeping silent about their plans wasn't right.

A groan rose to Will's lips, but he clapped a hand over his mouth. He must not be discovered here in the passage.

Stepping quietly and carefully, he made his way back to his bed, but he lay tense and wide awake.

He couldn't ignore what he had heard and allow the escape to take place. Even if no one ever discovered his part in it, *he* would know. He did not know how the council would react to an escape from the gaol. Perhaps his father might lose his occupation of gaoler and be disgraced. Then he—Will—would live with regret and self-blame his entire lifetime.

Squirming in bed, Will knew he must do what was right, no matter how much he dreaded it.

Since the next day was Sunday, Will did not have a chance to speak privately with his father until late in the afternoon.

During church services the beauty of the music his father played soothed Will and strengthened his resolve. "Will you come for a walk with me, Papa?" he asked afterward.

"I'll come with you," John interrupted.

"Me too!" Henry shouted.

"Not today, lads," Mr. Pelham said. He patted John's shoulder and ruffled Henry's hair. "I have things to talk over with Will."

Will darted a glance at his father. Could he possibly know what Will had in mind?

To Will's surprise, the streets were busier than usual on a Sunday, with more carriages than were common. "Why are all these people here?" Will asked in surprise as they began to walk down Nicholson Street.

"The General Court will soon be in session," Mr. Pelham said. "During Public Times people come— some to shop, some to discuss business, and some to attend the trials."

"But do not the laws forbid travel on Sundays?"

"Yes, but with the courts about to open, it is difficult for some people *not* to use Sunday for travel. 'Tis understood that exceptions can be made."

"Do you mean that sometimes a law is *not* a law?"

Mr. Pelham smiled down at Will. "A law is still a law. However, in some instances a law can be ignored. Does that confuse you?"

"Yes, Papa," Will said. How was this decision made? Who would be the one to make it? "It is almost too puzzling to think about."

"Then let us speak about other things. You will most likely be interested in the court sessions, where cases are tried."

"Will there be many cases, Papa?"

"Not too many. On Wednesday the court will hear the civil cases first. After the civil cases have been settled, the criminal cases will come to trial. All the cases tend to be heard quickly."

"What if the juries do not decide quickly?"

"Most do," Mr. Pelham answered. "The jurors are not allowed anything to eat or drink or to leave the jurors' chambers until they have reached a verdict. That law can help a man make a decision with little delay."

Will smiled as his father went on. "The opening of General Court will be very interesting, Will. It will begin in the Capitol with Governor Dunmore and the Council members taking their oaths as judges. They do this no matter how many times they have been sworn in as judges in other court sessions."

"It will be the first for Governor Dunmore," Will pointed out, "since he arrived in Williamsburg only a short time ago."

Mr. Pelham nodded agreement. "The governor and the councillors will then meet at Bruton Parish Church for a sermon. I'm certain the Reverend James Horrocks will give them an inspiring one."

Will often had a great desire to sleep when Reverend Horrocks's sermons grew too long, and he wondered just how inspired the governor and councillors would be if Reverend Horrocks had a great deal to say.

"After the sermon, everyone will return to the Capitol to begin hearing the civil trials," Mr. Pelham said.

"Papa, what will your job be?" Will asked.

"I must be on hand and ready to follow the commands of the court. I will bring the prisoners to court and keep them in custody until they are either acquitted or sentenced. Those who are acquitted will be set free. The others will be taken back to the public gaol to remain until their punishment is carried out. Those who are granted benefit of clergy I must punish at that moment before the judges of the court."

Suddenly Mr. Pelham paused, and Will knew he was thinking about having to cause pain to another.

"Papa," Will asked, "may I come to the opening session of General Court with you?"

Mr. Pelham brightened. "I was about to ask if you would like to attend. It would please me to have you at my side."

Will looked up at his father eagerly, but his joy changed to sorrow as he saw the desperation his father was trying so hard to hide. He took his father's hand and answered, "It would make me very happy to be with you, Papa."

How can I tell him now about my suspicions? Will wondered. The pressures on his father with the opening of the General Court and the dread of the punishment he might have to mete out would be difficult enough. Will couldn't add to these pressures.

But his father must be told.

"Papa," Will said, "what if a prisoner tries to escape? How will he be able to do it?"

"He won't," Mr. Pelham answered. "The keys to

the cells are either on my person or in your mother's pocket if I am not nearby."

Will felt a little better. "So if prisoners should talk about escaping . . ."

"It is nothing more than talk." Mr. Pelham stopped walking under a large maple tree, its red leaves a glowing canopy. "Why do you ask about escaping prisoners, son?"

Will thought carefully before he answered. "Jake said that Blackbeard is planning an escape. He hinted that Blackbeard will take Emmanuel with him. I think Blackbeard may be one of the other prisoners."

Mr. Pelham chuckled and continued to walk. "Old Jake is imagining things again. No one in our household—and that includes Jake's ghost of Blackbeard—would be able to put his hands on my ring of keys."

His answer satisfied Will, who happily trotted to catch up with his father. But early that evening, as he again brought water to the prisoners, Will could easily see that Emmanuel no longer seemed despairing, even though his owner would come for him in only four days. And Mills Mansfield accepted his cup of water with a grin, his eyes sparkling with excitement. Why?

Will promised himself to be ever on guard, to keep an eye on Toby, and to listen carefully to anything Jake had to tell him. No matter his mixed-up feelings, Will owed his father his sympathy and his loyalty. Will would do all in his power to make sure there would be no escapes from the Williamsburg public gaol.

During the daylight hours, Will shadowed Toby, rarely letting him out of his sight. He made it impossible for Toby to find time to speak with Emmanuel.

During the night, Will slept fitfully, fully dressed and with the door of the bedchamber ajar. A part of his mind remained alert for the possible creaking sound of a cell door's opening. He awoke often, each time lighting his candle and prowling the passage. He wanted any prisoners who were awake to hear him and know they were being well guarded. His father had said that no one would be able to put his hands on the keys, but Will wanted to make sure.

By Wednesday morning, he was exhausted. It was hard to climb out of bed in time to bring water to the prisoners and eat his own breakfast, but finally he dressed and was ready to leave with his father for the opening session of the General Court.

As he stood in the open doorway, adjusting his cocked hat, Will whispered, "Papa, where are the keys?"

His father patted one of the deep pockets in his waistcoat. "Here," he said. "Are you ready?"

I'm as ready as you are, Will wanted to answer cheerfully, but he couldn't—not when he saw his father's hands tremble and his eyes fill with concern for whatever might come.

Chapter Eleven

The formal opening of the General Court was every bit as grand as Mr. Pelham had promised it would be. For the first time, Will was close enough to get a good look at Lord Dunmore, and he was surprised at the governor's stern expression. Solid and stocky, Lord Dunmore did not smile or speak pleasantly to those around him, as his predecessor, Lord Botetourt, had. Instead, he seemed to look down his long nose at the Virginians who attended the ceremonies.

Will gave thanks that Reverend Horrocks's sermon was not as long as he'd feared. He did not disgrace himself and his father by falling asleep. Soon he was seated at the back of the courtroom in the Capitol, watching his father point out the clerk of the court;

the sheriff and undersheriffs; the cryer, whose duty it was to declare court in session and summon those whose cases were to be heard; the court chaplain, who would open each day's proceedings with a prayer; and the tipstaff, who served as messenger, usher, and doorkeeper. Most important, of course, were the governor and the Council members, who would sit as judges for each case.

Near the front of the room sat Thomas Jefferson, who, with his partner, George Wythe, was scheduled to represent the Nansemond County vestry and Church wardens who were trying to get rid of their minister for behaving inappropriately.

During the day there were many civil cases, in which Will's father took no part. Most of the cases were boring, and Will quickly lost interest.

On the other hand, Thomas Jefferson's case impressed Will. Although the argument involved church matters, Mr. Jefferson argued that the General Court did have jurisdiction, going back to the time when Christianity was introduced to Britain. Will realized the extensive reading Mr. Jefferson must have done to prepare his arguments. Even so, as Mr. Jefferson's speech grew longer and longer, Will had a difficult time staying awake.

When the long day was over, Will stumbled into the house and dropped into the nearest chair. His mother left the table where she had been preparing for their evening meal, and rustled to his side. Wrapping her arms around him, she said, "Dear Will, how good it was for you to attend the session today with your father. Did you find it interesting?"

"Some of it, Mama, but there were parts so slow I near fell asleep." Will yawned. "I want to attend the court tomorrow when the prisoners come to trial. I think Papa will want me to be there."

Mrs. Pelham smiled. "I am sure of it."

Suddenly remembering what he must do, Will tried to struggle to his feet. " 'Tis time for me to take water to the prisoners."

"Hush," his mother said, and she kissed his forehead. "The chore has already been done."

Will's eyes shot wide open in surprise. "Not you, Mama. Not the heavy bucket—"

"Of course not," she answered, and smiled. "I asked Toby and Nellie to do the chore."

Will was too shocked to answer. Toby had made contact with the prisoners! And Will hadn't been on hand to keep him from doing so. His mother had meant no harm by sending Toby to tend to the prisoners, but what if . . . ?

"Mama!" Elizabeth cried. "Help me! John keeps trying to snatch my doll!"

As Mrs. Pelham left to solve the argument, Will

hurried down the passage to the door of the men's cell. Looking through the barred window, he could see all the prisoners. John Watts, Samuel Flannagin, George Gray, and George Dutton were seated together, arguing about the merits of horses versus oxen in pulling wagons. Jake Sample and John King lay on heaps of the fresh straw, resting. Emmanuel stood at the outside window, staring through the bars. And Mills Mansfield, Colin Campbell, and Thomas Welch sat in a circle, flipping a coin and loudly betting on the outcome.

From where Will stood, the coin looked as if it might be a Dutch half gulden or a Spanish real. Will didn't stop to wonder to whom the coin belonged or how it had come into the owner's possession. He was too intent on making sure that Emmanuel was still wearing leg irons.

Satisfied that the conditions in the cell were normal, Will quickly went to his bedchamber, washed his face in the basin, and joined his family in the hall for supper.

He went to bed early, not caring about John's grumbling that he was not yet tired. Although Will remained clothed, the moment he lay upon his bed he fell into a deep sleep.

Will had no idea what time it was when something woke him. Had it been a voice? As he stood up he listened for the sound again, but there was only silence.

Alert, not knowing for what he should be prepared, Will left the bedchamber, slipped through the open door, and sat on the stairs in the darkness. He heard nothing more. Was the sound only in his dreams? The entire household seemed to be asleep and silent.

He began to rise, but the sound came again—from the men's cell down the passage. It was the repeated sharp scratch of metal against stone.

As Will jumped to his feet, he heard a crackle and saw a flicker of yellow light.

Frightened voices cried out from the cell. "Fire! Help! Take us out of here!"

Will raced down the passage, yelling for his father. When he heard his father's quick answer, he hefted the bucket of water that was always kept nearby. He saw that the fire was contained in an inside corner of the men's cell, where he could not reach it with the water, so he waited impatiently until his father arrived.

Mr. Pelham came running. He unlocked the cell door, grabbed the bucket from Will, and flung the water toward the blaze. "More water! Quickly!" he shouted at Will.

Will could see Sarah and Nellie struggling down

the passage with filled buckets. He took their buckets, handing them the empty one, then reached in turn for the buckets his father had just emptied.

"Mother has run to rouse the neighbors," Sarah shouted.

Mr. Pelham raced to unlock both the men's and women's outer cell doors, which opened into the high-walled exercise yard. "Outside, everyone!" he shouted. "Go into the yard! Hurry!"

In the hazy darkness, men stumbled and pushed toward the open door to the yard. Most were unrecognizable, except for Mansfield, his red hair gleaming in the light from the low bursts of flame. Will saw him bend over a much smaller man—Jake Sample—and help him outside to safety.

Someone ran past Will into the passage. "Toby, is that you?" Will shouted. "Bring water! We need more water!"

The blaze, which had been confined to a small heap of straw, crept forward, and the wooden floor of the cell began to smolder. As Sarah arrived with another full bucket, grabbing an empty one to refill, Will pulled off his shirt. He dipped it into the bucket, then slapped it against the small bursts of flames. "More water! Hurry!" he called to Nellie, who emptied her bucket on the fire and ran to refill it.

The cell reeked of scorched wood and wet straw.

121

Will could see tendrils of flame snaking out to flare up in new places. "We need more help!" Will yelled. "Toby! Toby, where are you? We need you!"

Clouds of smoke filled the cell, choking Will, nearly blocking his vision of the passage and the stairs.

John cried out, and Will froze in terror. "John!" he shouted. "Run downstairs to Mama! Quickly!"

A dark figure entered from the exercise yard, crossing the cell and heading toward the door that led to the passage. Recognizing the broad shoulders and flaming red hair, Will cried, "Mr. Mansfield, help my brother! I pray you! He's in the room upstairs!"

Mansfield hesitated.

As a silent look passed between them, the shirt Will had been using on the burning floor fell from his hand into useless tatters.

John appeared on the stairs, frightened and crying. Frantically Will tried to edge past Mansfield into the passage. "This way, John!" he called.

But his brother seemed confused. With a scream of fright, John suddenly turned and ran back into the bedchamber.

"Out of my way. You can't carry such a big lad!" Mansfield snapped. He pushed Will aside roughly and raced toward the stairs.

Mrs. Pelham, staggering under a heavy blanket that had been soaked in water, groped her way into the passage. She dropped the blanket and clutched Will's arm. "Where is John?" she shrieked. "He is not downstairs. Where is he?"

"There he is, Mama," Will cried out, pointing at Mansfield, who returned with John in his arms.

"Mama! Go outside!" Sarah screamed. "The smoke . . . the baby . . ." She and Nellie set down their heavy buckets and pulled at Mrs. Pelham.

"Calm yourselves and take the lads outside," Mansfield ordered. He thrust John at Mrs. Pelham and Sarah. To Nellie he said, "Bring more water."

Startled, they did what he told them.

Mansfield easily swung one of the buckets up in his arms and poured water on the burning wood.

In a few minutes Mr. Pelham returned. The prisoners were outside and safe. Volunteers who had heard Mrs. Pelham's alarm arrived and worked with the Pelhams until the fire was completely extinguished.

With blackened clothing, hands, and faces, the men who were crowded into the cell poked and prodded at walls and floor. "The structure itself is not harmed. The gaol can be repaired without trouble," one of them said.

Another felt the bars at the window. "No damage here. These will hold," he announced.

Will saw Mansfield quietly edge into the passage.

He caught up with him and said, "Thank you, Blackbeard."

Mansfield rested a hand on Will's shoulder. "No time to talk," he said in a low voice. "I must be on my way."

Will gasped as two neighbors, lanterns held high, entered the passage behind Mansfield.

As Mr. Pelham came from the cell to meet the men, he recognized Mansfield in the light from the lanterns. "Mansfield?" he asked. "You're a prisoner. What are you doing out here?"

"Papa," Will said quickly, "Mr. Mansfield rescued John and helped put out the fire. He was working to fight the flames right next to you."

One of the neighbors questioned, "He's a prisoner?" He leaned forward, squinting suspiciously at Mansfield. "Had you plans to escape? Did you set this fire?"

Before Mansfield could answer, Will shouted, "No! Mr. Mansfield could have escaped, but he didn't. He saved my brother John. Then he stayed to help put out the fire."

Will clutched his father's arm. "Papa, when Mr. Mansfield comes to trial, can you tell the judge what he did to save us? Can you ask for . . . ?" Will struggled to remember a word he had heard a lawyer use that morning. "For clemency?"

Mr. Pelham didn't hesitate. "Yes, I can," he answered. Looking into Mansfield's eyes, he said, "We are deeply grateful for what you have done, sir. I will indeed plead for clemency."

One of the neighbors stared suspiciously at Mr. Pelham. "Court is in session. You should have known there might be trouble. Did you not arrange for a night watch over the prisoners?"

Will spoke up. "*I* served as night watch," he said. "And—as you can see—that is why the fire was put out and did not spread throughout the building."

The neighbor took a step back, but he scowled at Mansfield. "You were in the cell. Tell us. Who set the fire?"

Mansfield shrugged. "I was asleep. The cell was dark. How could I know?"

Mr. Pelham stepped forward. In his hand were a hammer, chisel, rounded flint, and steel striker. Will recognized them as the tools kept in the cupboard next to the fireplace. Toby used the flint and striker to rebuild the fire in the hall fireplace whenever it went out.

The hammer and chisel must have been used to unlock Emmanuel's leg irons, and the striker to start the blaze that would cause the cell doors to be opened.

"Toby is missing, as well as the prisoner Emmanuel," Mr. Pelham said sadly.

Will's heart gave a leap. Emmanuel had escaped? Toby as well? Even though he was glad that Emmanuel had been able to leave before his cruel owner claimed him, Will found himself angry that Toby had left, too. Papa had always been good to Toby. Why had Toby deserted a good master and risked his life to run away with Emmanuel? If a slave helped another slave to escape, the penalty was death. Will remembered what Toby had said about freedom. Did freedom mean so much to him that he would risk his life?

Will watched his father and the neighbors lead the remaining prisoners to the empty debtors' cells. When the volunteers had left and the house had quieted, Will wrapped an arm around his father. "What will happen now?" he asked.

"I will be asked to explain what I can about the escape," Mr. Pelham said. "I may be reprimanded, but they most probably will not take any other action. I cannot be held accountable for one slave's helping another to escape."

"Do not worry about not having enough help since Toby is no longer here," Will said. "I can take on some of his chores."

"You are a good son, Will," Mr. Pelham told him.

"When the prisoners are tried, may I speak on behalf of Mr. Mansfield?"

"You will not be needed to testify. I will speak for him. I am fairly certain that because of his brave service tonight, even if he is found guilty of the forgery charge, his punishment will not be severe."

"Thank you, Papa," Will said. "I will be at your side."

Mr. Pelham smiled. "Then I shall be able to borrow some of your courage, Will."

Will smiled at his father in return. He hoped with all his heart that someday his father would earn enough money with his music to support his family and leave his position as gaoler. But until then Will would continue to do whatever he could to help him.

Epilogue

In the pause that followed the end of the story, Lori bounced in her seat. "Well?" she asked Mrs. Otts. "What happened?"

"To Mr. Pelham?" Mrs. Otts replied. "He served as gaoler until 1779 and as organist for Bruton Parish Church until 1802, when, at the age of eighty-one, he moved to Richmond. We know he was still giving music lessons until then."

Lori bounced again. "I don't mean what happened to Mr. Pelham. I mean the prisoners—especially Mills Mansfield and Jake Sample."

"And Margaret Turnbull," Keisha added.

Mrs. Otts closed her eyes for a moment as she thought. Then she opened them and smiled. "Jake was allowed to return to his farm," she said. "Margaret was

128

acquitted and released. Samuel Flannagin and Thomas Welch, who had been accused of horse stealing, were acquitted, too. Mills Mansfield was found guilty, but his punishment for that time was surprisingly slight. He was whipped and discharged."

"Was anyone else found guilty?" Stewart asked.

"Yes, indeed. Alice Field was sentenced to be imprisoned for one month and fined five pounds. John Watts was also found guilty of a misdemeanor. He was imprisoned for one month and fined twenty shillings."

Chip grinned. "I guess Mr. Pelham had at least four more weeks of John Watts's help at pumping the bellows for the organ in church."

"Unfortunately, the verdict for John King, who had committed a felony, was 'condemned,'" Mrs. Otts said. "The names of two other men, George Dutton and George Gray, are also listed with a verdict of 'condemned.'"

"What does that mean?" Lori asked quietly.

"We do not know. The records simply stated 'fate unknown.'"

Stewart said, "Well, at least Mr. Pelham didn't have to brand anyone in the hand in open court."

"Ah, but he did," Mrs. Otts told him. "You're forgetting Colin Campbell, who had been charged with the crime of maiming. He pleaded benefit of clergy and was burned on the heel of his thumb."

"Oooh! Gross!" Lori said, squirming, and Keisha groaned.

But Halim interrupted. "What happened to Emmanuel and Toby?" he asked.

Everyone quieted, their eyes on Mrs. Otts.

"Yes, what happened to them?" Chip asked.

"No one knows," Mrs. Otts answered.

"Then maybe Toby and Emmanuel made it to the west and to freedom," Halim said. "I hope they got away."

"I hope so, too," Lori said, and the others nodded.

Stewart stretched his fingers, studying them. "I like to play the piano, and someday I may want to be a musician," he said. "So I keep thinking how awful it must have been for a musician like Mr. Pelham to have had to work at the public gaol."

Mrs. Otts nodded agreement. " 'Tis certain many people are thrust into positions not of their own choosing," she said. "Like young Maria Rind, the daughter of William Rind."

"I remember his name," Lori interrupted. "Mr. Rind published the newspaper called *The Virginia Gazette.*"

"Yes, and when he died in 1773, Maria's mother took over his occupation of printer and publisher. It was very rare at that time for a woman to operate a business. Maria, who was only nine, found herself in charge of managing the Rind household and raising her healthy, noisy, rambunctious younger brothers while her mother worked long hours at the newspaper.

"The year 1773 was a time of great unrest—the year in which the Boston Tea Party took place," Mrs. Otts added. "More than anything else, Maria wanted to help her mother at the printing office, to learn to write news stories, and to print them."

"Why couldn't she?" Keisha asked.

"For two reasons. First, who else would have cared for the little ones? In 1773 cooking and cleaning were considered women's work, and Maria was the only girl in the family. And second, Maria had a secret, which . . . Ah, it's best not to tell that now."

Chip leaned forward. "What was it? You can tell us," he said. "We're listening."

Mrs. Otts's eyes twinkled as she said, "No, not now. 'Twill soon be dark. Maria's story is best told tomorrow."

"In the morning? Before the stalls open?" Chip asked.

"I'll be here waiting for you," Mrs. Otts answered. "Maria's story should be and must be told."

Author's Note

One of the most exciting parts of researching the lives of the children of Colonial Williamsburg is sorting through the facts that have been gathered about them and deciding what their personalities must have been like. What made them happy or sad? What did they love to do? Were they shy? Outgoing? Rebellious? Fun-loving? Quiet and reserved?

When I first read about Peter Pelham, I was shocked that a gentle musician would have to add the rough, difficult occupation of gaoler to his daily life. Did he dislike this way of earning a living? I think he must have, but he took the work because he had the responsibility of supporting his large family. Incidentally, the Pelhams' fourteenth child was a healthy baby girl, Parthenia, born in the spring of 1772.

What about Will Pelham, Peter's son, the boy I needed to know and understand? During the Revolutionary War, he served as a surgeon's mate, then a surgeon, in the Virginia hospital service. He continued working as a surgeon after the war, but in 1800 he suddenly changed his profession. He opened a bookshop and publishing house in Boston. Over the years he operated a circulating library and worked as editor of two newspapers: *The Ohio Republic* and *The New Harmony Gazette.* He was a scholarly man who loved books and who never ceased to study and learn.

Wouldn't Will, at the age of twelve, a creative person as was his father, have disliked his duties at the gaol as well?

I was sure that Joseph Hay, the son of Elizabeth Davenport Hay and Anthony Hay, had been a close friend of Will's. Born just a year apart, the two boys lived near each other and were both members of solid middle-class families. I had reason to believe that Joseph and Will carried their friendship into their young adult years, because Joseph, along with Will, was appointed surgeon's mate in the Virginia State Hospital at the commencement of the Revolutionary War. While no exact dates were given, it seemed as if Will and Joseph had enlisted together.

Suzanne Coffman, former editor at the Colonial

Williamsburg Foundation, brought to my attention Joseph's cousin Robert Greenhow, son of John Greenhow and Judith Davenport Greenhow. Three years younger than Joseph, Robert seemed to be a natural tagalong, so I included him in my story.

Peachy Davenport, who was Ann McKenzie's best friend in *Ann's Story: 1747*, was Joseph's aunt, so I enjoyed mentioning Aunt Peachy in the story, even if she appeared only behind the scenes, sipping tea.

Sometimes, as I read the historical records of people's lives sent to me from the Colonial Williamsburg Foundation's archives, I feel like a detective. Most of the General Court records no longer exist. But the October 17, 1771, issue of Purdie and Dixon's *Virginia Gazette* listed the cases heard by the General Court on October 16 and 17. According to this report, instead of being sentenced to death for the crime of forgery, or even being "burnt in the hand" as a result of pleading benefit of clergy, Mills Mansfield was given a relatively light punishment: "whipped and discharged."

This verdict was a surprise. What had Mansfield done to merit this favored treatment by judge and jury? I decided that Mills Mansfield was a character who would play an important part in Will Pelham's story.

The names of the other prisoners, their crimes,

verdicts, and sentences were taken from this list. I discovered that Colin Campbell did plead benefit of clergy, and his sentence was to be "burnt in the hand," so Peter Pelham, for the first time, had to carry out the sentence.

Jake Sample is the only prisoner who is an imaginary character.

It's recorded that Peter Pelham owned two slaves, but their names were not given, so I named them Toby and Nellie. I did not know the name of the imprisoned slave who engineered an escape, so I named him Emmanuel.

The fire set in the cell by the imprisoned slave escaping the gaol actually took place a few months after the time in which I set my story. We have no information about this man's future. Also, there was no recorded date for the escape of Pelham's slave or information that he was ever found. I took some artistic liberty and compressed time to include both of these events.

Peter Pelham served as gaoler from 1771 through the Revolutionary War. During the war the gaol became overcrowded with Tories, deserters, and other criminals. Research shows that because several prisoners escaped, the House of Delegates ordered an investigation into Peter Pelham's conduct. Mr. Pelham's friends came to his defense, pointing out that prisoners had escaped under the management of every single gaoler. The court must have agreed, because the House of Delegates voted not to discharge Mr. Pelham from his post as gaoler.

Records show that Thomas Jefferson was present at the sessions of the General Court in October 1771 and represented the plaintiffs in the civil case involving church matters. George Washington made frequent trips to Williamsburg that year. According to his diary, he came to Williamsburg at the end of October and very well could have been in Williamsburg at the Raleigh Tavern, so I included him in the story.

The year 1771 in Colonial Williamsburg was a time of relative peace between Britain and the colonists. However, the arrival of John Murray, fourth Earl of Dunmore, as governor of the Virginia colony would prove to be a problem. Lord Dunmore was every bit as unfriendly to and disdainful of the colonists as I depicted him and became one more stepping-stone in the path toward revolution.

About Williamsburg

The story of Williamsburg, the capital of eighteenth-century Virginia, began more than seventy-five years before the thirteen original colonies became the United States in 1776.

Williamsburg was the colony's second capital. Jamestown, the first permanent English settlement in North America, was the first. Jamestown stood on a swampy peninsula in the James River, and over the years, people found it an unhealthy place to live. They also feared that ships sailing up the river could attack the town.

In 1699, a year after the Statehouse at Jamestown burned down for the fourth time, Virginians decided to move the capital a few miles away, to a place known

The Capitol at Williamsburg

as Middle Plantation. On high ground between two rivers, Middle Plantation was a healthier and safer location that was already home to several of Virginia's leading citizens.

Middle Plantation was also the home of the College of William and Mary, today one of Virginia's most revered institutions. The college received its charter from King William III and Queen Mary II of England in 1693. Its graduates include two of our nation's first presidents: Thomas Jefferson and James Monroe.

The new capital's name was changed to Williamsburg in honor of King William. Like the Colony of Virginia, Williamsburg grew during the eighteenth century. Government officials and their families arrived. Taverns opened for business, and merchants and artisans settled in. Much of the heavy labor and domestic work was performed by African Americans, most of them slaves, although a few were free. By the eve of the American Revolution, nearly two thousand people—roughly half of them white and half of them black—lived in Williamsburg.

The Revolutionary War and Its Leaders

The formal dates of the American Revolution are 1775 to 1783, but the problems between the thirteen original colonies and Great Britain, their mother country, began in 1765, when Parliament enacted the Stamp Act.

England was in debt from fighting the Seven Years War (called the French and Indian War in the colonies) and believed that the colonists should help pay the debt. The colonists were stunned. They considered themselves English and believed they had the same political rights as people living in England. These rights included being taxed *only* by an elected body, such as each colony's legislature. Now a body in which they were not represented, Parliament, was taxing them.

A reenactment of Virginia legislators debating the Stamp Act

All thirteen colonies protested, and the Stamp Act was repealed in 1766. Over the next nine years, however, Great Britain imposed other taxes and enacted other laws that the colonists believed infringed on their rights. Finally, in 1775, the Second Continental Congress, made up of representatives from twelve of the colonies, established an army. The following year, the Congress (now with representatives from all thirteen colonies) declared independence from Great Britain.

The Revolutionary War was the historical event that ensured Williamsburg's place in American history. Events that happened there and the people who participated in them helped form the values on which the United States was founded. Virginians meeting in Williamsburg helped lead the thirteen colonies to independence.

In fact, Americans first declared independence in the Capitol building in Williamsburg. There, on May 15, 1776, the colony's leaders declared Virginia's full freedom from England. In a unanimous vote, they also instructed the colony's representatives to the Continental Congress to propose that the Congress "declare the United Colonies free and independent states absolved from all allegiances to or dependence upon the Crown or Parliament of Great Britain."

Three weeks later, Richard Henry Lee, one of Virginia's delegates, stood before the Congress and proposed independence. His action led directly to the writing of the Declaration of Independence. The Congress adopted the Declaration on July 2 and signed it two days later. The United States of America was born.

Williamsburg served as a training ground for

three noteworthy patriots: George Washington, Thomas Jefferson, and Patrick Henry. Each arrived in Williamsburg as a young man, and there each matured into a statesman.

In 1752, George Washington, who later led the American forces to victory over the British in the Revolutionary War and became our nation's first president, came to Williamsburg at the age of nineteen. He soon began a career in the military, which led to a seat in Virginia's legislature, the House of Burgesses. He served as a burgess for sixteen years—negotiating legislation, engaging in political discussions, and building social and political relationships. These experiences helped mold him into one of America's finest political leaders.

Patrick Henry, who would go on to become the first governor of the Commonwealth of Virginia as well as a powerful advocate for the Bill of Rights, first traveled to Williamsburg in 1760 to obtain a law license. Only twenty-three years old, he barely squeaked through the exam. Five years later, as a first-time burgess, he led Virginia's opposition to the Stamp Act. For the next eleven years, Henry's talent as a speaker—including his now famous Caesar-Brutus speech and the immortal cry, "Give me liberty or give me death!"—rallied Virginians to the patriots' cause.

Thomas Jefferson, who later wrote the Declaration of Independence, succeeded Patrick Henry as the governor of Virginia, and became the third president of the United States, arrived in Williamsburg in 1760 at the age of seventeen to attend the College of William and Mary. As the cousin of Peyton Randolph, the respected Speaker of the House of Burgesses, Jefferson was immediately welcomed by Williamsburg society. He became a lawyer and was elected a burgess in 1769. In his very first session, the royal governor closed the legislature because it had protested the Townshend Acts. The burgesses moved the meeting to the Raleigh Tavern, where they drew up an agreement to boycott British goods.

Jefferson, Henry, and Washington each signed the agreement. In the years that followed, all three men supported the patriots' cause and the nation that grew out of it.

Williamsburg Then and Now

Williamsburg in the eighteenth century was a vibrant American town. Thanks largely to the vision of the Reverend Dr. W.A.R. Goodwin, rector of Bruton Parish Church at the opening of the twentieth century, its vitality can still be experienced today. The generosity of philanthropist John D. Rockefeller, Jr., made it possible to restore Williamsburg to its eighteenth-century glory. Original colonial buildings

The Reverend Dr. W.A.R. Goodwin with John D. Rockefeller, Jr.

were acquired and carefully returned to their eighteenth-century appearance. Later houses and buildings were torn down and replaced by carefully researched reconstructions, most built on original eighteenth-century foundations. Rockefeller gave the project both money and enthusiastic support for more than thirty years.

144

Today, the Historic Area of Williamsburg is both a museum and a living city. The restored buildings, antique furnishings, and costumed interpreters can help you create a picture of the past in your mind's eye. The Historic Area is operated by the Colonial Williamsburg Foundation, a nonprofit educational organization staffed by historians, interpreters, actors, administrators, numerous people behind the scenes, and many volunteers.

Williamsburg is a living reminder of our country's past and a guide to its future; it shows us where we have been and can give us clues about where we may be going. Though the stories of the people who lived in the eighteenth-century Williamsburg may seem very different from our lives in the twenty-first century, the heart of the stories remains the same. We created a nation based on new ideas about liberty, independence, and democracy. The Colonial Williamsburg: Young Americans books are about individuals who may not have experienced these principles in their own lives, but whose lives foreshadowed changes for the generations that followed. People like the smart and capable Ann McKenzie in *Ann's Story: 1747,* who struggled to reconcile her interest in medicine with society's expectations for an eighteenth-century woman. People like the brave Caesar in *Caesar's Story: 1759,* who struggled in silence against the institution of slavery that gripped his people, his family, and himself. While some of these lives evoke painful memories of

A scene from Colonial Williamsburg today

our country's history, they are a part of that history nonetheless and cannot be forgotten. These stories form the foundation of our country. The people in them are the unspoken heroes of our time.

Childhood in Eighteenth-Century Virginia

If you traveled back in time to Virginia in the 1700s, some things would probably seem familiar to you. Colonial children played some of the same games that children play today: blindman's buff, hopscotch, leapfrog, and hide-and-seek. Girls had dolls, boys flew kites, and both boys and girls might play with puzzles and read.

You might be surprised, however, at how few toys even well-to-do children owned. Adults and children in the 1700s owned far fewer things than we do today, not only fewer toys but also less furniture and clothing. And the books children read were either educational or taught them how to behave properly, such as *Aesop's Fables* and the *School of Manners.*

Small children dressed almost alike back then. Boys and girls in prosperous families wore gowns

(dresses) similar to the ones older girls and women wore. Less well-to-do white children and enslaved children wore shifts, which were much like our nightgowns. Both black and white boys began wearing pants when they were between five and seven years old.

Boys and girls in colonial Virginia began doing chores when they were six or seven, probably the same age at which *you* started doing chores around the house. But their chores included tasks such as toting kindling, grinding corn with a mortar and pestle, and turning a spit so that meat would roast evenly over the fire.

These chores were done by both black and white children. Many enslaved children also began working in the fields at this age. They might pick worms off tobacco, carry water to older workers, hoe, or pull weeds. However, they usually were not expected to do as much work as the adults.

As black and white children grew older, they were assigned more and sometimes harder chores. Few children of either race went to school. Those who did usually came from prosperous white families, although there were some charity schools. Some middling (middle-class) and gentry (upper-class) children studied at home with tutors. Other white children learned from their mothers and fathers to read, write, and do simple arithmetic. But not all white children were taught these skills, and very few enslaved children learned them.

When they were ten, eleven, or twelve years old, children began preparing in earnest for adulthood.

Boys from well-to-do families got a university education at the College of William and Mary in Williamsburg or at a university in England. Their advanced studies prepared them to manage the plantations they inherited or to become lawyers and important government officials. Many did all three things.

Many middle-class boys and some poorer ones became apprentices. An apprentice agreed to work for a master for several years, usually until the apprentice turned twenty-one. The master agreed to teach the apprentice his trade or profession, to ensure that he learned to read and write, and, usually, to feed, clothe,

An apprentice with the master cabinetmaker

and house him. Apprentices became apothecaries (druggist-doctors), blacksmiths, carpenters, coopers (barrel makers), founders (men who cast metals in a foundry), merchants, printers, shoemakers, silver-smiths, store clerks, and wigmakers. Some girls, usually orphans with no families, also became apprentices. A girl apprentice usually lived with a family and worked as a domestic servant.

Most white girls, however, learned at home. Their mothers or other female relatives taught them the skills they would need to manage their households after they married—such as cooking, sewing, knitting, cleaning, doing the laundry, managing domestic slaves, and caring for ailing family members. Some middle-class and most gentry girls also learned music, dance, embroidery, and sometimes French. Formal education for girls of all classes, however, was usually limited to reading, writing, and arithmetic.

Enslaved children also began training for adulthood when they were ten to twelve years old. Some boys and girls worked in the house and learned to be domestic slaves. Others worked in the fields. Some boys learned a trade.

Because masters had to pay taxes on slaves who were sixteen years old or older, slaves were expected to do a full day's work when they turned sixteen, if not sooner. White boys, however, usually were not considered adults until they reached the age of twenty-one. White girls were considered to be adults when they turned twenty-one or married, whichever came first.

Enslaved or free black boys watching tradesmen saw wood

When we look back, we see many elements of colonial childhood that are familiar to us—the love of toys and games, the need to help the family around the house, and the task of preparing for adulthood. However, it is interesting to compare the days of a colonial child to the days of a child today, and to see all the ways in which life has changed for children over the years.

Crime and Punishment in the Eighteenth Century

The courts of colonial Virginia were modeled on the courts of England, with its laws, customs, and proceedings adapted to life in colonial America. In the early 1770s, Will's father, Peter Pelham, was keeper of the public gaol in Williamsburg and was required to live close to his job, in the gaoler's quarters. As gaoler, Mr. Pelham was an important court official and had many responsibilities. His main job was to imprison and care for people charged with or convicted of crimes.

The public gaol in Williamsburg was the prison for the highest court in the colony, the General Court, which met in Williamsburg at the Capitol four times a year. Prisoners in the public gaol might be charged with

The public gaol (pronounced like "jail") housed prisoners, as well as the court-appointed gaoler and his family.

misdemeanors or felonies ranging from theft to murder. Virginians could even be imprisoned for debt; and a debtor could be kept in prison for twenty days or more and have his belongings sold. Free people accused of capital crimes stood trial at the General Court in Williamsburg and awaited trial in the public gaol. If sentenced to hang, the prisoner stayed in the public gaol until the execution date. Runaway slaves like Emmanuel were held at the public gaol until their masters claimed them and paid their expenses.

The law required that Mr. Pelham publish a description of Emmanuel—and all other runaway slaves—in the newspaper for three months. If a slave remained unclaimed after three months, Mr. Pelham could hire him out to anyone in the area. Mr. Pelham would apply the money he received for the slave's work to the expense of keeping him at the public gaol and the cost of the advertisements. If the slave was still unclaimed after the charges had been paid and satisfied, Mr. Pelham could sell him at public auction.

Prison conditions in colonial days were cruel. Prisoners bedded down with only a thin blanket, even

Occasionally, prisoners wore specially made shackles forged at a blacksmith's shop.

on the coldest winter night. A diet of "salt beef damaged, and Indian meal" could not have been very appetizing. During the restoration of the public gaol in the twentieth century, archaeologists discovered shackles—grim evidence of the bleak life of a colonial criminal.

However, prisoners were allowed to talk with each other and to use the crude sanitary arrangements in each cell (the "thrones"), and those not charged with treason or a felony were allowed to walk about the exercise yard. In addition, the gaoler dispensed "physick," or medicine, when prisoners were ill. By law, the gaoler was required to take condemned prisoners to church. The local Anglican minister visited the condemned at the public gaol and accompanied them to the gallows.

Men and women accused of offenses stayed in the public gaol until their cases came to trial before the General Court. Serious crimes were punished harshly in the eighteenth century, and the death penalty was often carried out for offenses such as murder, arson, horse stealing, and piracy.

Will accompanied his father to the General Court to find out the fates of the prisoners. As Mr. Pelham explained to Will, the jurors usually made quick decisions because they were kept in a room without food and water until they reached a verdict.

First-time felony offenders, such as accused forger Mills Mansfield, might receive clemency, be granted

Death by hanging was a common verdict for felony crimes in Colonial Williamsburg.

a lesser sentence, or plead benefit of clergy. This one-time-only claim, which came from English law, was considered a humane alternative to the death penalty. If the court accepted a prisoner's plea, Mr. Pelham would brand his hand with a hot iron—"M" for manslaughter or "T" for certain forms of theft—forever marking the person a felon.

In the eighteenth century, various county officials, including sheriffs, subsheriffs, constables, and gaolers, were responsible for keeping the peace. Justices of the peace asked townspeople to help catch felons. The pursuit continued until the person was taken into custody or the chase abandoned.

The public gaoler would use a branding iron to burn the hand of a prisoner.

Captured criminals who were convicted received swift and severe punishment. Unlike today, time in prison was not often used as a punishment during colonial times. Gruesome physical punishments, such as public hangings, served as dramatic warnings against committing severe felonies. For lesser crimes—tried in lower courts—pillorying, whipping, branding, and mutilation in front of friends and neighbors often shamed criminals into better conduct. The lightest offenses usually resulted in fines. From fines to hanging, the punishment fit the crime, at least according to the mores of colonial Americans.

Colonial Williamsburg Staff

Recipe for Baked Apples

(12 apples)

Mrs. Pelham served baked apples as a dish at supper. In colonial Virginia, supper was a light meal served in the evening, while dinner was the main meal of the day, served around two or three in the afternoon. As was common practice in the eighteenth century, people used readily available ingredients, such as apples in the fall, to create fresh and delicious dishes.

12 baking apples
$^1/_4$ cup ($^1/_2$ stick) unsalted butter, plus extra to butter the baking dish
$^1/_4$ cup brown sugar
$1^1/_2$ teaspoons cinnamon
$^1/_4$ cup red currant jelly or honey

161

Preheat the oven to 350 degrees F.

Butter a 13 x 9 x 2-inch baking dish.

Core the apples. Trim away ½ inch of peel around the stem ends. If the bottoms are uneven, trim them so that the apples will stand upright. Place the apples in the prepared baking dish.

Place 1 teaspoon of butter, 1 teaspoon of brown sugar, ⅛ teaspoon of cinnamon, and 1 teaspoon of red currant jelly or honey in the center of each apple.

Bake at 350 degrees F for 40 to 45 minutes, basting the apples with the pan juices after 20 minutes. The apples should be slightly firm but tender.

From *Favorite Meals from Williamsburg,* published by the Colonial Williamsburg Foundation

About the Author

Joan Lowery Nixon is the acclaimed author of more than a hundred books for young readers. She has served as president of the Mystery Writers of America and as regional vice-president of the Southwest Chapter of that society. She is the only four-time winner of the Edgar Allan Poe Best Juvenile Mystery Award given by the Mystery Writers of America and is also a two-time winner of the Golden Spur Award for best juvenile Western, for two of the novels in her Orphan Train Adventures series.

Joan Lowery Nixon and her husband live in Houston.